"What as he p

Should Lillian tell him about the call? Or was she relying on him too much? She depended on him for her home. She shouldn't need his emotional support, too.

"Is it money?" he asked.

"No. I was telling Meena, Jonah's benefits have kicked in already. I just got off the phone with a lawyer working on Benny's case."

Brody slowed. "Did you learn anything?"

"No. They asked the same questions. I've answered them over and over. Why can't they leave me alone?" Her voice caught at the end.

"They're trying to get him prosecuted. Hang in there. You're here with us now. We aren't going to let anything happen to you."

Lillian turned her attention to her hands on the stroller handle. As much as she wanted to believe him, she couldn't. Because he'd emphasized *now*, reminding her she wouldn't be with them forever.

They didn't need her.

But she sure did need them.

Jill Kemerer writes novels with love, humor and faith. Besides spoiling her mini dachshund and keeping up with her busy kids, Jill reads stacks of books, lives for her morning coffee and gushes over fluffy animals. She resides in Ohio with her husband and two children. Jill loves connecting with readers, so please visit her website, jillkemerer.com, or contact her at PO Box 2802, Whitehouse, OH 43571.

Books by Jill Kemerer

Love Inspired

Wyoming Inheritance

The Rancher's Mistletoe Baby

Wyoming Legacies

The Cowboy's Christmas Compromise
United by the Twins
Training the K-9 Companion
The Cowboy's Christmas Treasures
The Cowboy's Easter Surprise
His New Companion

Wyoming Ranchers

The Prodigal's Holiday Hope
A Cowboy to Rely On
Guarding His Secret
The Mistletoe Favor
Depending on the Cowboy
The Cowboy's Little Secret

Visit the Author Profile page at LoveInspired.com for more titles.

THE RANCHER'S MISTLETOE BABY

JILL KEMERER

If you purchased this book without a cover you should be aware that this book is stolen property. It was reported as "unsold and destroyed" to the publisher, and neither the author nor the publisher has received any payment for this "stripped book."

ISBN-13: 978-1-335-62122-1

Recycling programs for this product may not exist in your area.

The Rancher's Mistletoe Baby

Copyright © 2025 by Ripple Effect Press, LLC

All rights reserved. No part of this book may be used or reproduced in any manner whatsoever without written permission.

Without limiting the author's and publisher's exclusive rights, any unauthorized use of this publication to train generative artificial intelligence (AI) technologies is expressly prohibited.

This is a work of fiction. Names, characters, places and incidents are either the product of the author's imagination or are used fictitiously. Any resemblance to actual persons, living or dead, businesses, companies, events or locales is entirely coincidental.

For questions and comments about the quality of this book, please contact us at CustomerService@Harlequin.com.

® is a trademark of Harlequin Enterprises ULC.

Love Inspired
22 Adelaide St. West, 41st Floor
Toronto, Ontario M5H 4E3, Canada
www.LoveInspired.com

Printed in Lithuania

And suddenly there was with the angel a multitude of the heavenly host praising God, and saying, Glory to God in the highest, and on earth peace, good will toward men.
—*Luke* 2:13–14

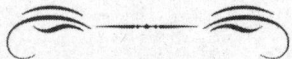

To my cousin, Jason Collard, for a lifetime of
fun memories. I will never forget the bean countdown!

To Shana Asaro and Rachel Kent
for making this series happen—thank you!

Chapter One

"Decision time." Brody Hudson carried the upside-down Stetson to his cousin, Hayden, sitting on the sectional in their late grandparents' living room in Fairwood, Wyoming. After Hayden dropped a folded piece of paper into their grandfather's hat, Brody sidestepped around the square coffee table and presented the hat to each of his siblings and cousins for their votes. When he set it on the coffee table, six sets of eyes were glued to it. "Who's going to tally the votes?"

His steady voice betrayed neither excitement nor fear. Ever since their grandfather died a month ago, Brody had been living for a dream. Roy Hudson had left Hudson Ranch Incorporated to the six of them. Their grandfather's remaining assets were in a trust to be divided equally between his two sons—their fathers, Bill and Tony Hudson—and six grandchildren. The papers in the hat would reveal their futures.

Would the third generation of Hudsons unite to run the ranch? Or would they resume their lives, sell the property and enjoy the financial windfall their grandfather had bequeathed them?

Brody wanted them to take over the ranch so badly he could taste it. But it wasn't only his decision to make. He glanced at his younger brother, thirty-year-old Cooper, and their baby sister, Meena—technically no longer a baby at twenty-seven. Cooper's resolute expression gave nothing away. Brody was certain Meena wanted to take over the ranch since she'd started renovating the cabins shortly after the funeral. He studied his cousins, Hayden, Seth and Kylie. Hayden's left hand clenched and unclenched, a sure sign of his nerves. Seth had the clear expression of a man willing to take a chance. The youngest of their crew, Kylie, was biting the corner of her lower lip. Meena scooched forward.

"I'll do it." With an eager gleam in her eyes, she placed the hat next to her and carefully retrieved each paper, unfolding and smoothing one on top of the other. Her shimmery pink nail polish highlighted the slowness of her actions. Brody wanted to yell at her to pick up the pace. His hair would be gray by the time she tallied the results.

Suspense built, burning through his core. He tried to distract himself by taking in the room, cozy as could be for the late October evening. Their grandparents' two-story house had five bedrooms, four bathrooms, a large sunroom and multiple areas for relaxing. The family had been calling it the lodge for as long as he could remember.

A fire blazed in the floor-to-ceiling stone fireplace at the center of the spacious living room. Behind the fireplace and to the right, a dining room held a long table seating twenty. An eat-in kitchen was in the rear of the house. And to the left was a den, where the six of them had spent many summer nights playing board games, bickering and laughing. They'd spent every summer together on the ranch until they'd grown up and gotten full-time jobs.

Although none of them had grown up in Wyoming, the land was in their blood. *Please, God, let the verdict be yes.*

"Well?" Hayden asked Meena.

Brody wanted to fist-bump him. Born a month apart, he considered his thirty-two-year-old cousin his best friend. If the votes were unanimous, Brody, the eldest of the grandkids, would be the CEO and oversee the corporation's enterprises, and Hayden would be the president and manage the daily operations of the ranch itself. The other four would be equal shareholders. Grandpa's ranch manager had agreed to run the place until they made a decision. After that, the sixty-eight-year-old was retiring.

Meena waited until she had everyone's attention. Her chin rose and her eyes sparkled. "Looks like we're moving to Fairwood! Six votes yes."

Brody's breath caught. Joy rushed through his veins. They all shot to their feet and began hugging each other. Only Cooper and Kylie refrained from whooping and hollering. He made a note to check in with them later. But for now? Time to celebrate!

After the excitement died down, they returned to their spots on the sectional.

Brody took charge. He always had. Always would.

"I was worried there for a minute." Brody pretended to wipe sweat from his forehead. "I can't tell you how glad I am that we're all on board. Personally, I'm ready for the six of us to live near each other. How many times did we say we were moving to Fairwood when we grew up? And now we're actually doing it. We'll get to see each other every day. This means more to me than you'll ever know. All because of Grandpa."

"To Grandpa!" they exclaimed.

Meena's eyes shone with unshed tears. Seth shook his head as if he couldn't believe it. Hayden repeatedly raked his fingers through his hair. Cooper appeared composed as always.

"It might take me a full year before I can move back." Kylie, the youngest, had been born five months after Meena. The girls were more like sisters than cousins. Cinnamon streaks ran through her long, dark-brown hair. She'd recently signed a lease on a one-bedroom in Cheyenne, where she worked as a certified nursing assistant. "I don't know what I'll contribute to Hudson Ranch. I doubt you guys need a CNA."

"We understand it's going to take time," Brody said. "This will be a big transition for us all."

Two weeks ago, the six of them had spent a long weekend here hashing out what an equal partnership would look like. They'd gotten advice from Grandpa's lawyer and agreed they would all move to Fairwood within a year if they all voted yes. Each of them could take their time figuring out a career path that best suited them. If it was something Hudson Ranch could invest in, all the better.

"Don't worry, guys, the cabins will be amazing." Meena held up her hands, palms out, and wiggled her fingers. At least she didn't yell "jazz hands," the way she usually did. "Brody, yours is done—thank you for giving me carte blanche on the decorating—and Seth, yours will be up next. Kylie, we have *a lot* to discuss before I begin yours."

"We'll go over the cabins' remodels later." Brody used his stern tone. Meena tended to get carried away with her enthusiasm for redecorating. After the funeral, she'd tasked herself with refurbishing all eight guest cabins on the property. She'd claimed her work-from-home job for an interior design firm in Texas wasn't hands-on enough for her taste. Brody had long since given up on reining in her impulsive decorating spurts. Their parents had indulged her whims, and he and Cooper went along with it—easier that way. "Practical matters first."

"Fine, but lose the attitude, or I'll add glitter and hot-pink accessories to your cabin." She pointed a long fingernail his way. "A disco ball, too."

"Noted," he said dryly. "Moving on. I'll tell the lawyer to go ahead with the paperwork. Now, let's review what we tentatively agreed to the last time we were here. The lodge will be the headquarters. Monthly meetings are mandatory—in person. Everyone can live in their cabin on the ranch, but no one has to. We'll consider adding businesses to our holdings as opportunities arise, but they will require a unanimous vote."

"Did we decide on what day to hold the meetings?" Seth typed something on his phone.

"Kylie and Cooper, what days work best for you?" They were the only ones with set schedules to work around.

Cooper pulled his shoulders back and had a determined glint in his eyes. "Don't worry about my schedule. I'll be here on whatever day you choose. It won't be for long—I'm moving here next spring."

"Perfect." Brody nodded with enthusiasm. With his experience assisting feedyards with cattle nutrition, Coop would thrive at Hudson Ranch. Tall and lean with black hair and pale blue eyes, he was the most reserved of the bunch.

"That's great, man!" Hayden said. "Will you miss your job?"

"I'm ready for something different." Coop shrugged. "I'm not sure what my role will be here. Looking for the right opportunity I guess."

Today just kept getting better. Brody could barely contain his excitement. "We could use your help evaluating the pastures and feed. Maybe you could do that for other ranches in the area, too."

"We'll see." Cooper looked away.

"Kylie, that leaves you. Any day better than the rest?" Brody asked. She'd have to fly back and forth. At least money wouldn't be an issue for her now that they all had fortunes from the trust fund.

"Thursdays. I'm working weekends, and I'll have Thursdays and Fridays off."

"Will the first Thursday of the month work for you, Seth?" Slightly shorter than Hayden, Seth had brown hair and brown eyes, while Hayden had darker brown hair and hazel eyes.

"Any day is fine." He shrugged. "I travel all the time, anyway. I'm booked with clients through January, but I plan on moving here soon after." Seth worked for a national company that trained service dogs. He'd always had an uncommon bond with animals.

"Okay," Brody said. "First Thursday of the month. Seth and Cooper will be moving next year. That leaves Hayden, Meena and me here for now. You're all coming for Thanksgiving and Christmas, right?"

Everyone assured him they'd be there.

"I'll see if Mom and Dad can get away from the lab for the holidays." Brody tapped his phone to add a reminder to call them tomorrow. Bill and Penny Hudson were obsessed with finding treatments for infections and diseases. Their research as world-renowned parasitologists took them around the globe. Their current gig in Peru was being funded by a government grant. They moved from place to place as their research called them. He couldn't remember the last time his parents had celebrated any holiday with him and his siblings.

"Don't bother calling them," Meena said. "I talked to Dad yesterday. They might have found a breakthrough with some weird worm. They're staying in Peru indefinitely."

No shock there. He was used to their parents bailing on them. He glanced at his cousins. "Do you guys know if Uncle Tony and Aunt Joanne will be around?"

"Mom told me they're hosting a donor event in Florida over Thanksgiving." Kylie rolled her eyes, shaking her head. "You know them—always fundraising for the university." Uncle Tony and Aunt Joanne lived on the east coast. Aunt Joanne was on the board of regents for a prestigious university, and

Uncle Tony worked in investment banking. They, too, rarely spent holidays with their kids.

The six of them shared knowing glances, and Meena let out a soft snicker. Cooper joined in. Kylie chuckled, and soon they were all laughing. Neither set of parents had wanted to live in Wyoming. That's why Grandpa Roy had left the ranch to the grandkids. His sons were wealthy and happy with their occupations. At the reading of the will, Bill and Tony had actually sighed in relief that they wouldn't have to deal with the ranch.

"How could our dads grow up here—riding horses, working cattle—and *not* want to do this every day of their lives?" Hayden asked. "I don't get it."

"I have no idea," Brody said. "It's hard to believe."

Seth shook his head. "All I did during the school year was dream about spending our summers here together."

"Remember the infamous pillow fight?" Kylie's eyes twinkled.

"Like any of us could ever forget." Seth's face lit up. "Grandpa yelled at Grandma to 'do something about those kids.' I don't think he expected her to join in."

"When he saw all the fun we were having, he couldn't resist grabbing a pillow, too." Hayden grinned. "Never thought I'd see the day that tough rancher would laugh so hard smacking us with pillows. That was the summer I always think back on. I thought those times would last forever."

"Me, too." Meena grew solemn. "And then we all grew up and moved apart."

"Now we have a chance to be together again. For good." Brody rose and stretched his hand, palm down, above the coffee table. Hayden stood, placing his hand on top of Brody's. Cooper joined. Then Seth, Meena and Kylie. They'd been a team for as long as they could remember. Every summer they'd ended their stay the same way. With a group chant.

"One, two, three—" Brody said, and they all shouted, "Wyoming forever!"

For the next hour, they discussed practical matters. Brody had a feeling there would be many sessions like this, and he didn't mind at all. For years he'd been biding his time, waiting for the opportunity to be his own boss. Becoming CEO of Hudson Ranch hadn't really occurred to him. He'd always figured Grandpa would bequeath the ranch to Brody's dad and uncle. Now that it was becoming reality, his mind spun with possibilities—to upgrade the buildings, to invest in businesses that would complement the cattle operation and to produce the highest-quality beef in Wyoming.

Later, when the fire died down, Meena and Kylie headed out with the promise they'd be back first thing in the morning. They were staying together in Meena's cabin down the lane. Seth and Cooper talked a few more minutes before going to their cabins, leaving Brody and Hayden alone in the lodge. They stood near the fireplace, where embers glowed orange on ashen logs.

"Have you had a chance to think about my proposal?" Brody asked him.

Hayden's forehead creased, a sure sign his natural tendency to overthink things had kicked in. It was the only real problem Brody foresaw. He and Hayden needed to build a working relationship in a short period of time. And while they were best friends, their personalities couldn't be more opposite.

Brody liked to take charge. Get things done.

Hayden liked to analyze things. To death.

"I have. And I think it's ambitious. Too ambitious. We need to get a feel for the current herd before we invest such a large chunk of money into a breed of cattle that might not do well in this part of the country."

Why couldn't Hayden trust him on this? "I've been studying genomics for years."

"I know, I know. You don't have to remind me about your degree in general ag."

"Don't forget the certificate in beef cattle range management." Brody's teasing tone didn't quite cover his annoyance. His experience working as a territory manager for one of the largest genomic operations in the world should count for something. If Hayden could get it through his thick skull that Brody was more than qualified to handle crossbreeding, they'd be able to produce the best beef around.

"How could I forget? You bring it up every time I see you."

"Maybe one of these times you'll realize I know what I'm talking about."

"I'm not questioning your expertise, Brody. I'm just saying we should get a solid feel for running this place before we take on an expensive commitment."

"But if we invest in—"

Hayden held up his hand. "Look, we're tired. We've dealt with a lot tonight, and we'll have plenty more to deal with tomorrow. Let's talk about it in another month when we've had a chance to settle in." Hayden clapped him on the shoulder and pivoted toward the hall to exit out the mudroom. "I'm going to bed."

Brody wanted to argue, but he held his tongue. Maybe Hayden was right. Maybe in another month they'd settle into a routine and Hayden would be more willing to listen to him. He hoped so.

The back door closed with a soft thud, leaving Brody alone in the lodge with his thoughts.

The earlier elation faded to a familiar melancholy. And

although he tried to avoid it, his thoughts went to Rebecca. What would she have to say if she were here? It had been over ten years since he'd last seen her. Her auburn hair and dancing green eyes would be forever etched in his mind.

How different this moment would be if they'd gotten married. He'd be wrapping her in his arms, lifting her off her feet, celebrating this new life...together.

What was she doing now? Probably married to some city guy. Two kids, a big house... Was she happy?

He closed his eyes, remembering the pain of her disappearing from his life without so much as a goodbye. Like he'd meant nothing to her. Like they hadn't been madly in love.

He'd better get some rest. After turning off the lights around the house, he verified the fire was out, put on his winter coat, locked up and walked onto the covered front porch. Snow was falling against the dark sky.

A figure approached. A woman carrying a bundle near her chest. Who would be out in this remote part of Wyoming on a night like this?

She reached the bottom of the porch steps.

Wait...he knew her.

"What are *you* doing here?" He crossed his arms over his chest as adrenaline pulsed through his veins. He hadn't seen her in ten years.

And she had some explaining to do.

"What are *you* doing here?" Lillian Splendor asked as she clutched the baby tightly to her. Not once during the drive had she considered that Brody might be there. When she'd hatched this plan, she'd even typed his name into a search engine, and the results had shown him living in Cheyenne. She remembered him telling her and Rebecca the tales of his childhood and how spending summers with his grandparents and cousins in Fairwood had been the highlight of his life.

Before leaving Omaha this morning, echoes of Brody's voice rang in her head, *My family would never turn away someone in need.*

Lillian had never been more in need than she was now. And she'd been in need plenty of times throughout her twenty-nine years.

"I live here." His tone had a menacing undercurrent, one she didn't recognize. But then, she'd known Brody when he'd been young, chivalrous and generous—everything a girl could want in a man. Rebecca had apparently stolen that from him, too.

Lillian shivered, not so much from the cold, but from an aching emptiness inside.

"I need to speak with your grandparents." She hoped she sounded coherent. At any moment, she'd fall apart.

"They're not here."

"When will they be back?"

"Grandma died almost ten years ago. Grandpa passed away last month."

Her mind reeled. Her last resort had just collapsed. Now what?

"What's going on?" His tone softened to one she recognized. Pent-up emotions threatened to bring her to her knees, but the dregs of her energy kept her standing.

"You always said your family would never turn away someone in need." Her voice had quieted to almost a whisper. Jonah stirred, and she lightly bounced the baby. Two months old today, the little darling.

"Come inside. Let's get out of the cold." He unlocked the door and held it open. She obeyed—too tired, too cold, too desperate to argue. "Have a seat."

"I need to change him." She hiked the diaper bag up on her shoulder.

Brody pointed to the left. "Bathroom's down the hall."

"Thanks." She hurried down the hallway. Brody had grown even more handsome over the years. He'd always been appealing in a rugged, cowboy way, but she'd never allowed herself to think of him like that. He'd been Rebecca's. Off-limits.

And if Lillian had known he'd be here now? She'd have driven a million miles in the opposite direction.

Once upon a time, she and Brody had been friends—back in college when he and Rebecca had been a couple. Lillian doubted Brody had any idea how much she and Rebecca had needed each other. He definitely didn't know the sacrifices Lillian had willingly made in response to Rebecca's choices.

They'd been foster sisters, best friends, roommates. Rebecca had been the only person Lillian could count on. They'd always had each other's backs.

And Lillian would be the first to admit that having Rebecca's back had meant hurting Brody, even if it hadn't been her intention. She wouldn't blame him if he told her to hit the road. She deserved it.

She made quick work of changing Jonah's diaper and washed her hands. Kissed his sweet cheeks, not ready to face Brody back in the lion's den—er, the living room. From the way Jonah's face was scrunching, the time had come to warm a bottle for him.

Hoping to find a kitchen, she continued down the hall. Bingo. She rustled for a bottle in the diaper bag. As soon as it warmed, she made her way back to the lion's den. Her back ached. Her legs ached. Her arms ached. But she mustered the final drops of her strength to join Brody near the fireplace.

"You have a baby, huh?" A hint of affection lifted the

corner of his mouth. Jonah's little legs kicked and his arms stretched.

"Sort of." How could she explain? Maybe she wouldn't have to. Maybe this nightmare called her life would right itself without her having to drag Brody into it.

"Why don't you sit down?" He motioned to the sectional, and she didn't need to be asked twice. Once she was settled, she shifted Jonah in her arms and offered him the bottle. He drank it with small gulps, and the sound soothed her weariness. Brody took a seat kitty-corner from her. "What's going on?"

What *wasn't* going on would be a better question.

"I don't know what to do." The events of the past four weeks weighed like concrete on her chest. "I have nowhere else to go." Admitting it pained her, but she didn't cry. She never allowed herself to cry.

"And you remembered to come here. After all this time." He steepled his fingers, tapping the index fingertips together. "What do you need?"

"If I could crash here for the night, I'll be out of your hair in the morning." Where she'd go, she had no idea. Her plan had always ended at Hudson Ranch with his grandparents showing her a spare bedroom and helping her figure out her options.

"What's going on?" His gaze probed. "You can tell me."

If she told him, it would hurt him. But if she didn't tell him, she'd have to get in her car and drive somewhere. It was late, she was exhausted, and she had Jonah to think about now.

"I lost my job. Got evicted. Someone hacked my bank account. I have six diapers left, and I've never been a mom. I don't know how to be a mom." She squeezed her eyes shut and practically choked on the lump in her throat. She never should have admitted all that.

To her surprise, Brody got up and sat beside her. He put his arm around her shoulders, hugging her into his side.

His strong arms, the faint scent of cologne, the warmth of his body—all had the same effect on her. She couldn't remember a time she'd ever felt so safe.

"Shh…it's okay." He caressed her arm. Made her think it really would be okay.

But it wasn't. Couldn't be.

Not for her.

She allowed herself a few more seconds of leaning against him, and then she straightened. The baby's eyelids drooped as he nursed the bottle.

"Stay here tonight," Brody said. "You and your baby can get some rest. We'll talk in the morning."

"That's the thing, Brody—" she spoke without hesitation "—this isn't my baby. It's Rebecca's."

Impossible. Brody scrambled to his feet. He turned away, rubbing his chin as he tried to grasp what she'd said. But he couldn't.

"Why do you have Rebecca's baby?" Saying her name out loud ripped open a wound in his heart.

"Because she named me legal guardian in her will."

The implications knocked, and reality settled like debris the day after a tornado.

"Rebecca's dead?" Had the wind been kicked out of him? He couldn't believe it. Wouldn't believe it. Rebecca—so full of life—couldn't be gone.

Lillian nodded, her attention on the baby. A deep sense of sorrow came over him. For all the anger he'd nurtured over the years, he'd never expected to mourn Rebecca.

He'd loved her. With every bit of his heart. And he'd known that he'd never fall in love again. Rebecca had taken his heart with her when she'd left him. He was no longer capable of trusting a woman with it.

"How?" He didn't want to know, but he needed to.

"We don't have to do this," she whispered.

"We do." He stared down at her, shifting his legs wide with his arms across his chest.

"She took a bad Adderall."

"A what?" He ran his hand over his hair. Began to pace near the fireplace. "The pharmacist should be brought up on charges."

"It wasn't from a pharmacy." Her messy black hair swished as she shook her head. "The Adderall was laced with fentanyl."

"You're telling me she didn't get it from a doctor?" He couldn't accept it. Lillian was wrong. She had to be.

"She started taking them in high school."

"But she had a prescription, right?"

"No. She had connections."

"Drug dealers." His world tilted. *Not Rebecca.*

Lillian's eyes were like the hot springs he and Hayden visited every year. As blue as could be. Clear. Honest.

"And the father? Why isn't he raising the baby?" He braced himself, not wanting to hear about Rebecca's amazing husband, but he'd be unable to live with himself if he didn't.

"She didn't know who the father was." The words came out thinner than his breath in frigid winter air.

Black market drugs. A baby with a stranger.

Everything he'd believed about Rebecca was turning out to be false.

"Tell me everything." He took a seat a few feet away from her. "From the beginning. From when she dropped out of college." When the spring semester ended, she'd moved without telling him where, and he hadn't been able to contact her.

She'd gotten a new phone number and blocked him from social media. That had hurt. Being so close, spending every spare minute together—only to be cut off with no warning. He couldn't remember a worse summer than that one.

With a strained sigh, Lillian took the bottle from the baby, now asleep, and set it on the coffee table. "I'll give you the short version. After we left college we moved to Omaha, Nebraska. We've been sharing an apartment there ever since. The pregnancy was unexpected. She had the will made, naming me the guardian, in her second trimester. After Jonah was born, she struggled. Maybe it was the lack of sleep. I don't know. But she took Adderall to keep her going."

He studied Lil more carefully. Purple smudges under her eyes. Sunken cheeks. Skinny—too skinny. A cloud of exhaustion, fragility and hopelessness surrounded her.

Questions chased each other. Why would Rebecca have a will made when the baby hadn't been born? Had she expected to die? Was the death an accident? And why had Lillian skipped the important parts—like why she and Rebecca dropped out of Kansas State University without telling him?

He didn't want to press her, not with her a sliver away from falling apart. But he needed more than what she'd given him. "And the rest?"

"I found her body in our apartment." He didn't miss the way her eyelids closed as if willing it out of her memory. "Jonah was crying. I... I tried to revive her. Called 9-1-1. I grabbed the baby and followed the ambulance to the hospital. While we were gone, our apartment was ransacked. Someone took my debit card and hacked into my bank account. Emptied it. I'm still fighting with the bank. The urgent care center where I worked shut down a week later with no warning. When I explained the situation to our landlord, he claimed we were behind on the rent. Rebecca promised me she'd paid it. I'm getting calls constantly from the police, the prosecutor and even the federal government about the guy who sold her the pills."

Brody grew calm as she spoke. Lillian seemed to be teetering on the edge of a nervous breakdown. She didn't know what she was saying. Rebecca would never have done all that. The baby must have been a one-time mistake with someone she thought she loved. And the Adderall? Another mistake.

He'd better get Lillian upstairs. Tuck her and the baby into bed. Let her get some sleep.

"Come on, Lillian. I'll show you to your bedroom. You can explain it all in the morning."

He hadn't expected the flames licking in her eyes. Why wasn't she happy? She needed help, and he'd offered it.

"Like I said, I'll leave first thing."

And deprive him of the truth?

"Get a good night's rest. We'll talk over breakfast. Do you have a suitcase in the car?"

She nodded.

"I'll go get it."

Tomorrow, he'd find out what really happened. And maybe he'd finally get some closure and be able to move on with his life.

Chapter Two

Jonah's murmurs woke Lillian the following morning. It took a minute to get her bearings. Warm blankets and a quilt covered her. The window revealed gray skies and falling snow. She checked her phone—7:04 a.m. She couldn't believe the baby had slept through the night. A first.

Now what? She couldn't stay at Hudson Ranch, but, oh, how she wished she could.

Impressions from last night returned. The house was even bigger than Brody had described it. And this room? Cozy, inviting, private. All the things she'd lacked growing up in foster homes.

In the portable crib, the baby stretched his chubby little arms by his ears. At least Rebecca had gotten that right. At the time, Lillian hadn't understood her manic frenzy to have a will made up—especially since the two of them had lived paycheck to paycheck and couldn't afford the extra expense—but Lillian had since chalked it up to God's providence. After Rebecca's death, Lillian had filed an official acceptance of the guardianship appointment with the courts. Jonah was legally her son now.

"I guess you're getting hungry, huh?" she said in a gentle, lilting tone. His cute face made all her problems disappear. Shifting to get out of bed, she shivered as her bare feet touched the floor. Then she grabbed clean clothes from her small suitcase, dragged a brush through her hair, picked up the baby and changed him into a fresh diaper and a fuzzy sleeper with puppy faces all over it.

She kissed the top of his head, tossed the diaper bag over her shoulder and opened the door. Looked both ways down the long hallway. Empty. Good.

With careful steps, she followed the aroma of coffee and made her way down to the kitchen. Brody must be up. The coffee hadn't brewed itself.

Tempted to pour herself a cup, she concentrated instead on warming a bottle, then took it to the large oval table in the corner. *Thank You, God, for getting us this far. I need Your help figuring out what to do next.*

"There you are." Brody beamed as he entered the kitchen. "Did you sleep okay?"

"Yes." She couldn't feel more awkward if she tried. This was Brody. The perfect guy. And Rebecca had rejected him, treated him terribly. Lillian's neck grew warm. She shouldn't have come here.

"Good." He went straight to the cupboard and took down two mugs. "Want a cup?"

"Yes, please." Relief that he'd offered drew her attention to her empty belly. She dared not ask for something to eat, too. Never assume you could have what was right in front of you—a lesson she'd learned as a child moving from foster home to foster home.

"Cream? Sugar?" After pivoting to the biggest refrigerator she'd ever seen, he opened the door.

"Both."

He wore jeans and a sweatshirt today. They hinted at his muscles. He could have been a football player with those broad shoulders. He brought over a plate with pastries and muffins, then went back to the counter and returned with their mugs. He sat across from her and took a drink.

The air crackled with unspoken words. She eyed the banana muffin, the steaming coffee and then the baby.

"When was the last time you ate something?" His head angled slightly.

"I don't know." She couldn't remember. She'd stopped for gas yesterday afternoon, hoping her credit card wouldn't be declined. Before that? Ah...yes. The night before last, she'd packed everything she could fit into her old Kia Optima, polished off the leftovers from a box of macaroni and cheese, forced down half a can of expired peaches and tossed an opened bag of stale generic cereal into a tote for the road.

The cereal would come in handy later this afternoon when she and Jonah were on their way.

"Eat." The word was more than a command. It was permission.

She selected the banana muffin and took a bite. Food had tasted like sawdust ever since finding Rebecca's dead body. But this muffin? Bursting with flavor and moist. Delicious. She had to force herself not to devour the entire thing.

After shifting Jonah to her other arm, she took the first sip of coffee. It, too, tasted better than any coffee she'd had in weeks. She took another drink, a bite of muffin and hoped Brody wouldn't ask her any questions.

"I'm sorry you're going through a hard time."

Still kind. Still caring. How she envied his relaxed posture. She didn't know how to respond.

"Last night you were pretty upset. Why don't you walk me through everything again?"

Walk him through what? The worst night of her life? The subsequent haze she'd been in as she tried to deal with blow after blow?

"What do you want to know?" She still had a few bites of muffin left. Jonah was quiet as he nursed the bottle.

"Her death." He stared into the mug, then at her.

"I already told you." She'd shared the entire horrible tale. What more could she add?

"You said Adderall and fentanyl."

She nodded, opening her eyes wide for emphasis. What was he getting at? His lips drew together as his eyes narrowed. Didn't he believe her? Why would she lie about it?

"Did she have a job?"

"Yes. She bartended."

His eyelashes fluttered in shock. "Bartended?"

"Made good money at it, too. Well, she used to when she worked for the country club. After she quit, she worked at a chain restaurant and didn't make as much." Lillian still wasn't convinced Rebecca had quit the country club. More likely, her erratic behavior had gotten her fired. It had happened more than once over the years.

Brody's cheeks flushed. Lillian had always been good at reading body language and undercurrents. He was upset. And why wouldn't he be? She braced herself. Ever since coming face to face with him last night, she'd known there'd be a reckoning.

His cheeks puffed out as he exhaled. "You're telling me that Rebecca—funny, kind, generous Rebecca—worked as a bartender, bought prescription drugs from some guy off the street, had a baby out of wedlock, didn't know the father and died from an overdose?" His voice grew louder, higher as he spoke.

"Yes."

"I don't believe it." He shook his head, refusing to meet her eyes. "You must have her mixed up with someone else."

Gratitude warred with irritation. She was thankful that

even after all Rebecca had put him through Brody was giving his ex the benefit of the doubt. No wonder Rebecca had loved him. But Lillian's irritation overrode it. He And he was basically calling her a liar.

Why was he putting Rebecca on a pedestal even now? The benefit of the doubt seemed to exist only for his ex.

Shame brought a bitter taste to her mouth. What did it matter?

Rebecca had been more than a best friend. She'd been the only family she'd ever known. And they hadn't even been blood related.

"You didn't know her like I did." The coffee had reached the ideal temperature—not too hot, not too cold—and she took a long drink. Jonah lost interest in the bottle, so she set it on the table and lifted him to burp him.

"I knew her." His expression hardened. His voice did, too.

"The woman you knew in college was only one side of her." She didn't want to argue with him. She also didn't want him accusing her of not being honest. The rhythm of patting the baby's back helped calm her nerves.

His lips parted as if to contradict her, but something sad clouded his eyes, and his tension visibly dissolved.

"She was more than the summary you gave." Lillian wouldn't let him reduce Rebecca's life to a sordid paragraph. "She was fierce and loyal. Larger than life. She made me laugh. Would have given me the shirt off her back and the shoes from her feet if I needed them. I loved her. She was all I had. And she's gone."

"I needed her, too. I loved her, too." He knocked his knuckles on the table. "And she's been gone from me for over a decade."

And that's why she couldn't stay at Hudson Ranch.

"Thanks for letting me crash here, Brody." She drained

the last of the coffee and clutched the baby as she stood. "I'll be on my way."

"Wait. What will you do?" His forehead creased. "Where will you go?"

"I'll figure out something." She jostled the baby as she took a step, but Brody stood and blocked her path.

"Take a seat so we can discuss this."

She stared into his chest, only inches from her, then looked up into his eyes.

Concern emanated from him. Concern for her.

Whoa. Impossible.

"Please?" He gestured to the chair she'd abandoned. Jonah reached for her pinkie, gurgling as he grasped it. She sat once more with the creeping sensation this would only prolong the inevitable—her leaving.

"The other things you mentioned last night—" he rubbed his chin "—about your apartment and bank account and the investigations. Tell me more."

Like she wasn't embarrassed enough already. "I'm going to need more coffee."

"I'll take care of it." He took her mug, and soon, a full cup of coffee was in her hand. Brody made himself comfortable in the chair.

"Rebecca met Benny Tatter a few years ago after Frank was arrested. Frank had been getting her the Adderall before Benny. I didn't know she'd found a new supplier, but I lived with Rebecca long enough to know when she was taking stimulants. She'd go through cycles. Happy, full of energy to the point of being manic, then down and depressed. I tried to convince her to get help. She said she didn't need help. When she got pregnant, I was sure she'd quit. And she did. For a while."

Lillian hated remembering the past twelve months of walking on hot stones, treading carefully, knowing for a fact she'd get burned.

"After Jonah was born, everything fell apart. She became irrational. Maybe it was postpartum depression or lack of sleep. I don't know."

"Why didn't you force her to get help?"

A dry chuckle burst from her mouth. "Force Rebecca? No one could force her to do anything."

That shut him up. For the moment.

"What happened to the apartment?" he asked. "The break-in was while you were at the hospital, right?"

"Yeah. I think Benny saw the ambulance and waited for me to leave. He trashed our apartment, looking for evidence against him."

Brody muttered under his breath.

"I don't know if he stole my debit card or if it was someone with him, but like I said, my account was drained." Her fingers trembled thinking about it. She and Rebecca always helped each other cover expenses. The baby had taken most of their combined resources. But the remaining money in her bank account would have gotten her through a couple of weeks at least.

"The police—they arrested the guy?" Brody's jaw shifted. "Benny, you said?"

"Yes. He got out on bail." She decided not to mention that he'd threatened her.

"Did he bother you?"

"Define bother."

He sat up straighter. "What did he do?"

"The police are handling it. The state's prosecuting him, and the Feds are involved now, too."

"What about the money?"

She made baby faces at Jonah to avoid eye contact with

Brody. The money was a problem, hopefully resolved soon. "The bank took ten business days to investigate, but then they wanted written confirmation of the error. I provided it last week. I'm calling them today to see what's going on."

"And your job?"

"I was a medical receptionist at an urgent care for five years. We heard rumors about hospitals consolidating, but we didn't expect our center to shut down with no warning."

"I'm sorry, Lillian. You've had too much put on your shoulders in a very short amount of time."

Emotions rose, and she struggled to push them away. She didn't know what to do with sympathy. It would be a mistake to get used to it.

"Thanks, Brody. Thanks for listening, and for breakfast—"

"This isn't breakfast."

She'd eaten a muffin. She hadn't imagined it, had she?

"That was a snack. I'm making real breakfast now. Eggs, bacon, hash browns, toast. You stay there, and I'll have a plate for you in no time."

"You don't have to do that. Really." Her defenses crumbled, not at the thought of eggs and bacon and all the rest, but at him caring enough to offer.

"I want to." His lips curved upward, making his brown eyes shimmer. Oh, boy. That could be a problem.

The sound of the front door opening startled her. She'd assumed only Brody was staying on the ranch. Footsteps approached. Male footsteps if she had to guess.

"Hey, man, where's breakfast?" A tall, athletic man with brown hair entered the room. Lillian guessed him to be the same age as Brody. He halted when he spotted her. "Oh. Hi."

"This is my friend, Lillian. We knew each other in college." Brody said it nonchalantly, as if the past ten years hadn't happened. "Lillian, meet my cousin—Hayden."

"Nice to meet you." Hayden approached with his hand out. She shook it, and he sat sprawled out and loose-limbed in the chair Brody had abandoned. "What brings you to Hudson Ranch?"

Where to start?

Brody held a skillet. "She's staying here for a while."

"No, I'm not." In one hour, she'd be miles away.

"Great. We'll show you around. Do you like horses?" Hayden arched his eyebrows. Had neither of them heard her? "Who's this little guy?"

"His name's Jonah."

"He's cute." Hayden half rose, leaning forward to see him better, and smiled.

"Thank you." She caressed the baby's hair away from his forehead.

Noises from the front of the house warned her more people had arrived. She should have escaped when she had the chance. Now she'd be stuck here through breakfast—admittedly, she needed a fortifying meal—and would have to wait to figure out a plan later. What that plan would be, she had no idea. But being around Brody for long was not going to work. She'd leave as soon as she could.

"Do I smell bacon?"

"Extra crispy. I know how you like it." Brody's spirits rose as soon as Meena and Kylie entered the kitchen. They'd provide a welcome distraction from Lillian's revelations.

He was too emotionally caught up in the past. He probably shouldn't have put up a fight to keep Lillian here. But something had compelled him to. Guilt? Worry? Years of conditioning to help anyone in need?

"Oh!" Meena halted. "I didn't know we had a guest. I was wondering whose car that was in the driveway."

"This is my friend Lillian Splendor." He pointed the spatula toward Lillian. "The baby's name is Jonah."

Meena and Kylie rushed over to introduce themselves. He listened with half an ear. They'd keep Lillian from driving away while he cooked. If she left now, he'd lose contact with her and the baby the same way he had with Rebecca. Maybe that was the reason he wanted her to stay for breakfast.

Something deep inside him balked at losing Lillian, too.

Brody cracked eggs into a mixing bowl as Seth and Cooper entered the kitchen. More introductions were made. He glanced over his shoulder at Lillian. Her cheeks had a pink tint missing before now, and the corners of her blue eyes crinkled at something Cooper said. Kylie was holding Jonah near her face and talking to the baby in a singsong voice.

He whisked the eggs and poured them into a skillet, checked on the hash browns and yelled to Hayden to brew more coffee.

"How long are you staying?" Meena's voice cut through the chatter. Brody peeked at Lillian. She shrank into herself.

"Not long."

"A few days?" Meena traced the rim of her empty mug and turned to Hayden. "Are you brewing more coffee or do I have to?"

"I'll do it." His chair scraped the floor as he pushed it back. "None of us can handle you on only one cup. I'd rather face a mountain lion. Our apologies, Lillian."

Meena wadded up a paper napkin and threw it at him. It bounced off his back.

"Didn't hurt." He drew close to Brody. "So what's going on with—" he whispered, jerking his thumb toward Lillian.

"Later." Brody did a quick shake of his head. "I'm trying to convince her to stay a few days."

Understanding crossed Hayden's face. He rubbed a few

coffee filters to separate them and then yelled, "Looks like you're stuck with decaf, Meena."

"What? No!" Meena jumped out of her chair and rushed over to him, stretching on her tiptoes to search the cupboard for coffee. She pulled down a full bag of medium roast and shoved it into Hayden's chest. "Next time look harder. Decaf is nothing to joke about."

He grinned, then whispered something near her ear that Brody couldn't make out. Her face transformed the way it did when she'd latched on to a mission. Brody shuddered. He'd seen that look on his sister's face many times over the years. She was plotting something.

"What are you two whispering about?" Seth joined them.

"Nothing." Hayden backed up with his palms out near his chest. "Just making coffee."

"Want me to make the toast?" Seth asked.

"Yes, please." Brody continued scrambling the eggs.

The running faucet drowned out what Kylie and Lillian were discussing, but Brody strained to listen anyhow.

"...why don't you stay through the weekend?" Kylie was saying, with Jonah cradled to her chest. Appreciation for his cousin filled him.

"I really have to get going," Lillian said.

"Where to?"

A tap on his shoulder made Brody miss her reply. Hayden pointed to the bacon. "Are you going to flip those before they burn?"

"Oh!" He turned down the burner and turned each piece as quickly as possible. "Thanks, man."

"Distracted, huh?" The knowing expression on his face made Brody want to take a paper towel and wipe it off.

"Make yourself useful. Get out the plates and silverware."

Hayden mock-saluted him. Living around each other would

take some getting used to. Brody had forgotten how chaotic the summers used to be. Living on his own in Cheyenne and traveling to various ranches for his job had given him independence. In another week, he'd resume his role as leader of the pack. Was he up for it? Would they resent him?

"Do you know where Grandpa kept the Christmas decorations?" Meena leaned against the counter, staring at him. "I need to go through everything and start getting this place ready for Christmas."

"It's still October."

"For one more day. Do you know where they are or not?"

"Probably in the attic. I'll check later."

"Promise?"

Hayden nudged her out of the way. "Leave him alone. He's got important stuff to do—those hash browns require the perfect amount of crisp."

While the two of them bickered, Brody turned off the burners.

"Breakfast is ready." He placed the strips of bacon on a paper-towel-lined platter, scooped the scrambled eggs into a serving dish and left the hash browns in the skillet. "Let's pray before we eat."

Everyone grew silent and bowed their heads.

"Lord, we thank You for bringing us together and for our new venture together. We ask that You bless Hudson Ranch and this food. And bless Lillian and Jonah, too. Amen."

The conversations resumed as everyone fell in line to fill their plates. Lillian, holding Jonah again, hung back, and Brody went over to her.

"How are you doing?" He took the opportunity to study her. Dark circles under her eyes, arms like toothpicks even with a sweater covering them, gaze darting around the room like a cornered animal.

"Good. I'm good." She licked her lips, clearly fibbing. "What did you mean when you prayed? What's the new venture?"

"Last night, before you arrived, we all agreed to take over Hudson Ranch as equal partners."

Her mouth curved up, making her look younger, and he couldn't help noticing how pretty she was with her medium-length black hair, pale skin, blue eyes and full lips. "Wow, that's incredible. Congratulations."

"Thanks." It still didn't seem real. He couldn't wait to get started. "We're excited about it. I'll be CEO of the company, and Hayden will manage the ranch itself."

"What is the company?"

"It's actually a corporation that includes the ranch. We're looking to add more businesses in the future."

"Like what?" She slowly swayed with the baby, who yawned and snuggled into her embrace.

"We're not sure. It depends on what my siblings and cousins want to do. Everyone has their own set of talents. We're hoping everyone finds their calling here."

"What's yours?"

"I'll tell you—but first, let's grab some food." He took her by the elbow and gently steered her toward the counter. Seth was layering jam on a slice of toast. Everyone else had gotten their food and found spots at the table. Good-natured chatter filled the kitchen. "I'll make your plate. Your hands are full."

"You don't have to—"

"I want to." He selected two plates. "Eggs? Bacon?"

"Everything."

"That's what I like to hear."

After he'd loaded the plates, he carried them to the table, where two empty seats remained next to each other. He proceeded to tell her about his current job and how he was putting in his notice. Then he went over how he and Hayden planned on checking every inch of the ranch and determining what needed upgrading around the property.

"You'll do great." Her voice sounded wistful.

"Are you okay?"

She nodded quickly, but he didn't miss the sorrow in her eyes. Here he'd been going on about his life upgrade after she'd admitted to being crushed with Job-like calamities. "Hey, what Kylie said earlier? She's right. You should stay here a few days."

"I can't." She shook her head rapidly.

Kylie craned her neck around Cooper. "Lillian, listen to Brody. We want you to stay. Call me selfish, but I am obsessed with babies. I could gobble little Jonah up!"

"She's not lying," Hayden said. "Obsession is an understatement. You'd be doing us all a favor by staying. If she's occupied with Jonah, she can't force us to play Pictionary."

"You're just mad because we always beat you." Meena held up her mug to Kylie for air cheers. Kylie did the same.

"I figured out long ago to always be on their team," Seth said, taking another bite of toast.

"We almost won last time." Cooper glared at the girls.

"Almost. Remember that, Coop. *Almost.*" Meena shot him a saucy look.

"What do you say, Lil?" Brody asked. The oddest sense of anticipation came over him. He still cared about the friend he'd made in college. He'd lost Lillian, too, when Rebecca disappeared from his life.

"I don't know. I'd better not. I'm low on supplies, but it was nice of you to offer." Her eyebrows furrowed together.

"Seth's running to the store this morning. He'll get whatever you need." Brody gave Seth a just-go-with-it stare.

"Yeah, we're running low on cucumbers." Seth's startled

expression made Brody want to roll his eyes. He couldn't come up with something better than cucumbers?

"See?" Brody drew his lips together in a tight smile. Would she buy it?

"I guess I could stay another night," she said weakly.

"Great." Triumph surged through him.

"I'm going with Seth to the store," Kylie said. "Just give me your list, Lillian. He won't know what to do in the baby aisle if you need anything for Jonah."

"I'll go with you." Meena carried her empty plate to the dishwasher. "Give me a few minutes to get ready."

Kylie went to the junk drawer and grabbed a pen and small pad of paper. She set them on the table in front of Lillian. "Here you go. Write what you need. Leave it there when you're done. If you want to take a shower, I'll watch Jonah for you." She held her arms out to take the baby.

Lillian hesitated. Then she handed him to her. "Thank you. I'll be quick."

"Take your time." Kylie cradled him, smiling down at his content face. "He's so sweet."

Lillian scrawled a short list of items. Then Brody told her where she could find the towels, and she left the room. When she was out of earshot, everyone grew quiet and stared at him.

He rose. Should have known they'd all demand an explanation. In their shoes, he'd do the same.

"I met Lillian at Kansas State. She was Rebecca's best friend." A murmur rippled around them. "The three of us spent a lot of time together."

"Is this the same Rebecca who broke your heart?" Cooper's expression grew hard.

"Yes." As if he'd gone around dating other Rebeccas.

"And you're okay with her being here?" Hayden seemed curious about the whole thing.

Last night, no. Today? Yes. He didn't know why.

"Rebecca died. Jonah is her son." He noted their eyes widened, and a few mouths formed O's. "Lillian's going through a rough patch. I appreciate you all making her feel welcome."

Kylie's eyes glistened. "If Jonah is Rebecca's son, she must have died recently."

"About a month ago." The tightness in his throat returned. He wasn't sure why her death was affecting him so much. "Lillian's pretty torn up about it, so I hope you'll respect her and not ask too many questions."

"Not even about the father?" Meena whispered loudly.

"The kid doesn't have one."

"Sounds like Lillian could use some support." Hayden met Brody's gaze and nodded. "We're here for you. And for her. Whatever you think is best."

Brody handed Meena Lillian's list. "Buy triple anything she has on there, and throw in anything you think she might need for herself. I'll pay for it."

"Like what?" Meena folded the note and tucked it into her pocket.

"I don't know. Girl stuff. You and Kylie should be able to put your heads together and come up with something."

"We'll take care of it." Kylie smiled at the baby, then addressed Meena. "Why don't you get ready? I'll stay here with the baby. Then Seth and I can pick you up from the cabin before we head out."

"You have half an hour," Seth said sternly. "Not one minute more."

Meena glared at him. "You act like it takes me hours to get ready."

Seth and Kylie exchanged loaded glances.

"Fine. Thirty minutes." Meena left in a huff.

"You up for a horseback ride?" Hayden asked Brody. "Now

that we know this place is ours to run, I want to go over every square inch of it."

"I'll have to take a rain check on that." Brody itched to tour the ranch, too, but he couldn't be certain Lillian wouldn't take the baby and leave if he was away. He didn't want to trap her here, but her fragility worried him.

God had led her to Hudson Ranch for a reason, and Brody didn't want her on the road until she got some rest and had some money in her pocket. In the meantime, if he could learn more about why Rebecca left him, he might get some closure. He just wasn't sure he could handle the truth.

Chapter Three

This was getting ridiculous. Sunday morning, Lillian folded Jonah's clean clothes in her bedroom at the ranch. Since arriving three days ago, she'd made sure her bags were packed and the diaper bag was ready to go each night. And every morning, she'd give herself a pep talk to leave. She couldn't take advantage of the Hudsons' hospitality another minute.

But every day the six of them would convince her to stay a little longer.

She'd never been a pushover. Why couldn't she say no to these people?

Because you need them.

Friday afternoon, Kylie and Meena had presented her with bags of supplies and goodies for her and Jonah. They'd obviously stretched the truth when they told her Seth had thrown everything in the cart, and they hadn't had the heart to hurt his feelings by putting it all back. Lillian had told them she couldn't accept it. They'd waved her off with chuckles.

Later the girls had given her a tour of the cabins and pointed out the ranch's outbuildings. Jonah, bundled in his fleece snowsuit, had bounced in her arms, clearly loving the great outdoors. Brody had offered to join them, but Meena and Kylie had told him to go ride around the ranch with

Hayden—that the tour was for girls only—and Jonah. Hearing them boss around Brody had been fun.

She'd never been on a ranch. She'd asked them if it was normal to have so many guest cabins, and they'd both laughed. Apparently, it wasn't. Their grandmother had been born into a wealthy family and had inherited a fortune. When her grandchildren were still small, she'd insisted on having the cabins built, anticipating a future with her grandchildren and their families staying for extended visits. She'd told them she wanted them to have their own space. That way they'd stay longer.

Lillian placed a clean sleeper on top of the pile in her suitcase and picked up the final onesie to fold. She'd never imagined a family like Brody's actually existed. Sure, she'd tucked away his descriptions of summers with his family, but she'd mostly clung to the promise he'd told her and Rebecca over and over again. *"My grandparents would never turn away someone in need."* He'd even scrawled out the ranch's address on index cards for them both. It had touched Lillian that he'd made a point of including her. She'd slipped her card into a file with important documents, never dreaming she'd make use of it one day.

The contrast between the way the Hudsons had grown up and the way she and Rebecca had grown up couldn't be more striking. As far as Lillian knew, she had no siblings. Rebecca didn't either. Lillian only had one memory of her mother. She'd been three years old when she'd stumbled across her dead body and screamed at the top of her lungs until someone arrived. Her mother had died from a drug overdose.

The first foster placement had been for a year, and if she had any memories of it, they were vague. Every twelve to eighteen months, her social worker, Brenda Sansor, would stop by and help her gather her things into a garbage bag.

Then they'd drive to a fast-food joint, chat over burgers and head to her new home. The foster homes shared common traits—multiple kids, little supervision and all in a poor area outside Kansas City. She'd met Rebecca when she was ten.

No use thinking about it now. She zipped the small battered suitcase shut. A knock on the door made her sigh. *Lord, give me the strength to leave this time.*

"Come in," she said, glancing at Jonah, sleeping in his bouncy seat near the window. With everyone's help caring for the baby the past few days, she'd been able to gather her thoughts. She no longer had the panicky terror she'd arrived with. It had mellowed into an uneasy anxiety. Another good thing? On Friday, she'd found out the bank had restored the money to her account.

Now she had options. What they were, she didn't know, but at least she had money again.

"Hey, I wanted to talk to you about something." Brody came in and crossed over to the window. He smiled tenderly at Jonah before turning to her.

"What is it?" She had to be strong. She wouldn't stay another day.

"Everyone's leaving this afternoon."

"Oh." A new fear spread through her body. They expected her to leave. She hadn't given their plans much thought. Of course, they had jobs to get back to. *Think, Lil.* She'd spent an hour researching the area last night. A cheap hotel on the outskirts of Fairwood would work for a day or two.

"Hayden and I are moving here later this week. In the meantime, we want you to stay in one of the cabins."

They wanted her to stay? They weren't kicking her out?

"Why?" There had to be an ulterior motive in there somewhere.

"Because Meena's been here on her own for the past couple of weeks, and we'd feel better if she wasn't alone."

Meena seemed pretty independent. Lillian doubted she minded being alone.

"I know she doesn't need a companion or anything." Brody shifted his attention outside the window. Another gray day out there. Then he addressed her again. "The ranch hands live in town, and it would take them twenty minutes to get here if anything were to happen."

"What do you think is going to happen?" She genuinely wanted to know. What exactly worried Brody about Meena being alone?

He tilted his neck forward, massaging the back of it with one hand. "She's up and down on ladders all the time. Painting. Decorating. And contractors have their crews in and out of the cabins throughout the day. My sister's beautiful. What if someone gets ideas? Sees she's alone with no one around to help her?"

Lillian could relate to that. His fears came true all too often in her world. Just one of the reasons she and Rebecca had lived together. For their safety.

If she viewed Hudson Ranch as another foster home, she could probably stay a week. Like her former placements, the ranch would be a temporary arrangement. She'd have a safe place to stay and time to come up with a plan. It sure beat driving to a dive motel for the night.

"When did you say you were moving in?" She rubbed her forearms absentmindedly.

"I'll be here Friday night. The movers are delivering my stuff on Saturday."

"Will you live in the big house?"

"The lodge?" His eyes danced. My, he was handsome. She'd better not think along those lines. Would only get her into trouble. "No. We're all moving into our cabins. The lodge will be our headquarters, though. Guests will stay there, too."

"What about when you have a family of your own? Where will you live then?" She found it hard to believe Brody wasn't married already. The guy had *family man* written all over him.

"I'm never going to have a family." The words were as hard as marble. As cold, too. "When Rebecca cut me out of her life, I learned a valuable lesson. I'm not trusting anyone with my heart again. I'll live and die alone."

The unexpected words shocked her. "You can't mean that."

"Oh, I do." His eyes flashed with bitterness and finality.

Maybe it was for the best he'd be gone all week. The questions he'd inevitably want to ask would remain unspoken, and she'd avoid having to share the hard facts about her and Rebecca's lives. Even if she explained how they'd been brought up—laid everything out for him—she couldn't see him truly understanding. Not when he'd been raised with people who loved him.

"What about you, Lil? Why aren't you married?"

"Me?" She half scoffed, half chuckled. "Are you serious?"

He blinked twice. "Yes."

"I suppose I'd have to date someone for a while before that could happen. I don't see a husband in my future."

"Why not?"

The few blind dates Lillian had been on hadn't impressed her. Besides, men didn't notice her. For as long as Lillian could remember, guys only had eyes for Rebecca. It used to bother her, but she'd accepted the fact they couldn't help falling for her gorgeous, charismatic bestie.

And now her bestie was gone.

"I don't think I'll find a man who's faithful and willing to stick by me when life gets rough. Besides, I'm kind of a wallflower." Men were drawn to luscious red hair and Hollywood charm.

"That's not true." He squinted as if she didn't have a clue. "You're pretty. You're not a wallflower."

She ducked her chin, overcome with confusion at his words. He considered her pretty? She'd always thought of herself as forgettable.

"Plus, I have a baby now." Hunching her shoulders, she perched on the edge of the bed. "I've never been wife material. I'm not even mother material."

He came over and sat next to her with his arm brushing hers. It sent a streak of awareness over her. "Don't say that."

"Why not? It's true. I don't know what marriage or parenting is supposed to look like." She'd been winging it each day with the baby. At some point, she'd have to figure out what being a good mother entailed.

"You're doing an amazing job caring for Jonah. You're a natural."

Hope rose. "You think so?"

"I know so." He patted her hand and stood. "Listen, if you decide to stay, don't worry about expenses. I already made arrangements with Fairwood Supermarket to charge anything you order to my account."

"I couldn't do that. My bank account is back—"

"Save it for Jonah." He gave her a don't-argue-with-me look. "You'd be doing me a favor by being here. I don't want it to cost you anything out of pocket, okay? What do you think? Will you stay?"

"Until Friday?"

"Saturday. I'll probably be arriving late Friday night."

She weighed her options. Remain here where she had shelter, food and a place to regroup? Or leave with no real plan?

"I'll stay. Thank you. Don't worry, I'll be on my way first thing on Saturday."

"I hope not. You don't need to rush."

That's where he was wrong. She did need to rush. Or she'd get caught up in the false safety of being with his family and be blindsided when they got tired of her.

Only this time, she wouldn't have Brenda Sansor to pick her up, buy her a burger and drive her to a new home.

One week. And she'd be gone.

In less than fifteen minutes, the ranch would be his permanent home. As Brody drove under a sky full of bright stars Friday night, he reviewed the decision he, his siblings and cousins—he'd been thinking of them as the squad—had agreed upon yesterday.

They all wanted Lillian and Jonah to stay on the ranch indefinitely—for as long as she wanted.

On Wednesday, he'd set up a video call with the squad to explain, without going into too many details, what Lillian had been through after losing Rebecca. They'd fallen into a stunned silence. Kylie had insisted on sending Lillian information to apply for social security dependent benefits for Jonah. Seth had asked if Brody thought she might need a therapy dog. Brody told him he didn't know. Cooper had followed up by telling him to urge her to live on the ranch in their parents' cabin. Hayden had seconded that it would be for the best. Meena had been thrilled with the idea of Lillian staying on the ranch indefinitely.

They'd all agreed Brody would be the one to invite her to live there. For that, he was thankful.

He'd known Rebecca and Lillian had been best friends growing up, but until Lillian had arrived last week, he hadn't grasped that Lillian had no family. And no family meant not having anyone to turn to in times of trouble.

Had Rebecca been in trouble when she quit college? If so, why wouldn't she have turned to him?

It had been a decade ago. He needed to put it behind him. He'd done his best to push her from his mind over the years, always with the promise he'd never give his heart to anyone else. But Lillian had unlocked the gates to his past. He kept wondering what had gone wrong. What had he missed back then?

The driveway appeared with log poles on either side and the Hudson Ranch sign swinging overhead. His truck wound down the drive, past the lodge to the lane that led to the cabins. After parking next to his, he cut the engine and paused to gather his thoughts.

His siblings and cousins were full of compassion and generosity—that's why they wanted Lillian to stay. But Brody? He didn't have the same pure motives.

Sure, he sympathized with Lillian's predicament. He held no ill will toward her, only gratitude for their revived friendship. He'd like to think the main reason he was asking her to stay was unselfish. But two truths kept overriding it.

One—he was drawn to her honesty. He found it easy to be real with her. He always had. And two—he wanted answers to decade-old questions.

He got out and slammed the truck door. Cupped his palms to his mouth as the frigid air assaulted him. Early November and cold as Antarctica. He took in the circle drive and all eight cabins. Meena must have gotten a head start on decorating for Christmas. Every porch had strings of lights wrapped around the posts and wreaths on the front doors.

After grabbing his bags from the back seat, he strode up the porch steps of his cabin, unlocked the front door and went inside. In the entry hall, he yanked off his cowboy boots and padded forward to the living room. The hardwood floors held an oval area rug, and a leather couch and matching recliner faced an entertainment center with a massive television. The art Meena had chosen felt right. He particularly liked the watercolor painting of a cowboy on horseback riding away toward the mountains. Meena had instructed the contractors to add dimmable canned lighting that made the cabin brighter than he remembered.

He moved his bags to the bedroom, opened the fridge—empty—and checked his phone. No texts. No missed calls.

Was ten o'clock too late to check on Lillian?

He'd just mosey over to her cabin. Knock quietly. Make sure she was okay.

With his boots back on and leaving his coat unzipped, he made his way down the curved portion of the circle drive to his parents' cabin—Lillian's temporary digs—and knocked softly, hoping he didn't wake the baby.

A few moments later, she opened the door a crack, a questioning look on her face. When she saw it was him, she smiled and let him inside.

The two-bedroom cabin was larger than his but similar in style. Meena hadn't renovated it yet, but it didn't feel outdated. A massive dog slept on the rug in the living area.

Where had that beast come from?

"Sorry to barge in," he said softly, not sure if Jonah was sleeping.

"I'm glad you made it back safely." She gestured for him to sit in the plush, gray recliner and sat across from him on the matching couch, tucking one leg under her bottom.

"Me, too, and this time it's for good." Saying those words was like honey to his soul. He'd dreamed of this moment—

making Hudson Ranch his permanent home—since he was a young boy. "Where's Jonah?"

"Asleep in his porta-crib." She pulled a throw over her lap as she shivered. "Are you excited about moving here or nervous?"

"Excited. I've been wanting to move here most of my life."

"I'm not surprised. I always enjoyed hearing about your childhood adventures here."

"You remembered?" He discreetly studied her. Her cheeks had a healthier glow than last time he'd seen her, and she didn't seem as close to a breakdown, either. Maybe the ranch was doing her good.

"Of course." She looked taken aback. "It sounded like something you'd read about in a novel. Helping your grandfather with the horses. Learning how to rope calves. Riding horses everywhere. Playing games with your siblings and cousins."

"Your summers weren't like that, huh?" He treaded lightly, not wanting to offend her.

She averted her eyes. "No. They were far from it."

The dog thumped its tail, stretched out on all fours and ambled over to Brody, sniffing his legs.

"Who's this?" He let the enormous dog sniff the back of his hand before petting its head. The tricolored fur was soft.

"Oh, that's Butch. He showed up on Monday. Meena talked to the ranch hands. He belonged to Junie Blackstone."

"Why is Butch here and not with Junie?"

Lillian cringed. "Junie died. Butch had nowhere else to go. He wandered over, and Meena said the ranch could use a good watchdog."

Brody wasn't convinced of the dog's watchdog abilities, considering he hadn't woken when Brody walked in. But the happy-looking canine seemed to be right at home.

"Saint Bernard?" he asked, scratching behind its ears.

"Bernese mountain dog."

He'd have to research the breed later. Find out how they were with cattle. A good herding dog was worth its weight in gold. Something told him this dog wasn't much of a herder, though.

"How did your week go?" he asked. "Did my sister drive you bonkers?"

Lillian picked up a mug—hot tea from the looks of it—and held it between both hands. "Of course not. She's the best."

"The best? If you say so." It pleased him she liked his sister, but he'd never admit it. Would only get back to Meena and make her ego even bigger than it already was.

"Brody, I have something to run by you, and I don't want you to be upset." She took a sip and set the mug down once more. Her blue eyes brimmed with worry. He hoped the bank hadn't given her more trouble. Had that deadbeat drug dealer found her? If that guy had been harassing her...

"Kylie sent me information about applying for benefits for Jonah—social security benefits."

He relaxed. Kylie had told him all about it.

Lillian swallowed. "She and Meena told me to use the ranch's address since I don't have one."

He waited for her to explain the problem. Had the social security office turned her down or something? She stared at him as if expecting him to reply.

"And?" he asked.

"You're not upset I used your address?" Her forehead wrinkled as if she couldn't fathom it.

"Why would I be? I'm glad you used the ranch's address. In fact, I talked it over with everyone, and we think you should stay here."

"Stay?" She blinked in confusion.

"Yeah. My parents don't need the cabin—they never come to the ranch. You and Jonah can live here. You'll have your own place. And privacy."

"I'm sorry, Brody, but I'm not following."

What part was confusing? He thought he'd spelled it out. "We want you and Jonah to live here. On the ranch. Here, in my parents' cabin. For as long as you want."

"Like a week or two?"

"No, Lil. Like a year or two."

Seeing her shocked face flooded him with long-forgotten memories. Of sitting with Lillian in the library, waiting for Rebecca to show up. Of standing in line at the dining hall, talking about studying for finals. Of her handing him a birthday card and him being touched that she'd remembered. Of there being no awkwardness between them. Ever. They'd been tied by Rebecca—and they'd both been happy with it.

Being friends with Lillian had taken no effort at all. She'd been easy to talk to, a great listener. A good friend.

He'd missed her, too. And he wanted her friendship back.

Lillian had entered another universe. It was the only explanation.

Brody seemed to be expecting an answer, but she couldn't believe he actually meant it. He wanted her to stay on this haven of a ranch? Long term?

Being here had given her much-needed rest. All week, she'd enjoyed quiet mornings in bed, feeding Jonah his bottle and cuddling him. Her afternoons were spent with Meena, watching her work in Seth's cabin. They'd talked about life. Meena had asked her opinion about what kind of decorating each cabin needed. Lillian wasn't qualified to say and had told her so more than once. Still, it had been nice to have a girlfriend to talk to again.

Alone with Jonah in the cabin each night, she'd thought about her future, and last night she'd made the decision to ask Brody if he'd be okay with her settling nearby in Fairwood.

She needed a safety net, and the Hudson family could provide it. Not that she'd abuse their generosity. She didn't *want* to ask them for anything. Ideally, she'd get in her car and start over somewhere new without a second thought. But she had Jonah now.

Lillian would never put him through a childhood like hers. And that meant she needed to find the right job, a good babysitter and a cheap apartment. Fairwood was as good a place as any to start over.

"I know it's a big decision," he said, still petting the dog.

"I don't know what to say. I didn't expect it." Maybe she should have. Brody had included her since the day he met Rebecca. He was the kind of guy who refused to let someone be left out.

"I have to warn you." He grew serious. Her stomach plunged. *Here it comes. You knew it was too good to be true.* "When everyone moves here, it's going to be chaotic. Seth and Cooper will be arriving in a few months. While I love Hayden, he's worse than Eeyore when it comes to thinking about the future. Always seeing the downside. And Meena, well, you've seen for yourself her creative energy. It can be exhausting. Seth's not much of a talker. Kylie, obviously, is."

Temptation seized her. The temptation to get to know his family, to be part of it—even as an outsider. How she'd longed for a family her entire life! But no matter what she'd done, she'd been rejected.

"I don't know. It's very generous of you. But I—"

"Think about the baby, Lil."

The warmth in his gaze brought down her defenses. Before she could change her mind, she nodded. "I'll stay. I'll help out around here. And pay rent—I'm working on getting a job—but it might take me a while to find one."

"No rent. The cabins need to be heated during the winter or their pipes will burst. It doesn't cost us a thing for you to live in one. Don't worry about rushing out to get a job, either. The baby needs you. And you could use some rest after everything you've been through."

Had every dream she'd ever had come true in this moment?

"I'll pay you back," she whispered.

"Didn't you hear me?" He straightened. "Keep your money."

She knew of only one other way to repay him. The price would be high. Maybe too high. But she owed it to him.

"Whatever you want to know about Rebecca—all you have to do is ask," she said. "I'll tell you anything."

His face paled, and he turned to stare at the fireplace. A moment passed. Then he looked at her with an intensity that made her shiver.

"I might take you up on that."

Lillian never offered anything she wasn't willing to give. Sooner or later, Brody would start asking, and she'd have to tell him the difficult things in her past. Because Rebecca's past and hers were intertwined and had been since the day they met.

She hoped it would be worth it.

Chapter Four

If Grandpa could see him now, he'd be proud. Not just of him, but of all six of them. For taking a chance and keeping the ranch going.

The following morning, Brody rose before dawn and saddled one of the horses. Shaggy, a palomino stock horse, had quickly become his favorite during his time on the ranch since the funeral. He directed Shaggy down the trail toward the far pasture. The cold air held no snow. His lined leather gloves kept his hands warm enough. Pink and orange spread up the horizon. Sunrise at Hudson Ranch. Nothing more beautiful in the world except maybe sunsets at Hudson Ranch.

What would his grandfather have done about Lillian?

He'd have encouraged her to stay. And the baby, too.

Brody relaxed into the horse's slow gait as he surveyed the frost-tipped pasture. Their grandfather had been a thoughtful, hardworking, pragmatic man. He'd tended to see beyond external circumstances to the heart of a person.

Could Brody say the same for himself? How had he missed all of the internal issues Rebecca had clearly been dealing with when they'd dated? And what exactly had he seen? Apparently, only what she'd wanted him to.

Vibrant, warm personality, exciting to be around—she'd brimmed with vitality. Rebecca had attracted people to her like bees to honey. She made them feel special—she'd made *him* feel special.

Since then, none of the women he'd met through work, mutual friends or church had sparked even a passing interest on his part. He hadn't wanted to be interested, anyhow.

But with Lillian here...she'd been on his mind ever since she'd arrived.

Probably just sympathy for her on his part. Boy, she'd been through a lot.

He dismounted and opened the gate to the pasture, led Shaggy through, closed it, then got back in the saddle and rode toward the cattle in the distance. With tails flicking and a chorus of moos, the cattle grazed. None of them scattered or flinched as he approached the first group.

Every cow, bull, heifer, steer and calf had been recorded in Grandpa's ledgers, going back for decades. Hudson Ranch had focused on the Hereford breed due to their calm, friendly personalities and ability to adapt to harsh environments. Their red-and-white coloring made them easy to identify. In recent years, Grandpa had invested in a small herd of Black Angus cattle, but he kept them in a separate pasture. Brody intended on changing that soon.

He had a list of changes he was ready to make. He wanted to upgrade the outdated ledger system to a blockchain ledger software with digital tags. Plus, he planned to crossbreed Simmental cattle with the Herefords to increase their heat stress resistance and promote their growth rates. Sure, it would be a major expense, but he was passionate about keeping up with the times.

Convincing Hayden of all of this wouldn't be easy.

Brody would prevail, though. Of that he had no doubt.

The sky was the limit when it came to this ranch, and he fully intended on bringing it to maximum potential.

Shaggy skillfully maneuvered through the cattle, and the animals barely looked up as they munched on prairie grass. All the preg checks had been done recently. Brody would have to consult Hayden on what to do about the cows that weren't pregnant. But that could wait for another day.

He and Shaggy slowly made their way through the herd, checking on cows and occasionally treating any with obvious health issues. By the time he'd finished a few hours later, his muscular frame ached from being in the saddle, and he had a sense of fulfillment of being his own boss, living out a dream, doing what he'd always felt meant to do.

After he'd brushed and taken care of Shaggy, he strode to the big red barn where the ranch's office was located. A man he guessed to be around his father's age stood next to a late-model truck with his hands in the pockets of his dark wool jacket as he gazed at the sky.

"Can I help you?" Brody approached him.

"I hope so." His clean-shaven face had a gentle warmth. He thrust out his hand. "Sonny Armstrong. I grew up on this ranch."

That was news to him. He shook the man's hand. "Brody Hudson. I live here now." He almost added that he was the CEO of Hudson Ranch Incorporated but figured it would be overkill.

"You must be one of Bill or Tony's sons. My father, Jeff, was your grandfather's right-hand man until Dad passed away unexpectedly when I was twenty."

"It's good to meet you, and I'm sorry for your loss." Brody vaguely recalled seeing pictures of Grandpa and Jeff together. One photo had them riding horses next to each other. Another showed them roping calves. "Grandpa spoke highly of your dad."

Sonny's face fell slightly. "With good reason. He was a stand-up guy."

Brody waited for Sonny to give him a hint of why he was there. The cold began to seep through this clothing. When the man didn't speak, he extended his arm toward the barn. "I was heading into the office. Care to join me? It's heated. We can get out of the cold."

He nodded, and neither spoke until they'd settled into chairs inside the office. Another thing Brody would need to bring into this century. The large room had an old desk, a beat-up table, filing cabinets and a couple of chairs. It smelled of coffee, dust, cows and hay. The most advanced technology in the office was an ancient calculator with paper tape for printouts.

"What brings you this way, Sonny?" Brody clasped his hands on the desk.

"Prayer. At least, I think that's what brought me here." He looked embarrassed. "I've spent the past forty years as a chef. I've worked all over the world. The older I get, though, the more I miss my dad. I miss Wyoming. I miss the simplicity of life on Hudson Ranch."

Brody nodded but wasn't sure what to say.

"I've been living in Fort Lauderdale, executive chef of a restaurant there, and last month, on a whim, I did an online search for Fairwood, Wyoming. The first thing that popped up? Roy Hudson's obituary. I knew God was telling me something. I made a few calls—I went to high school with Fairwood's mayor, Glen Brown—and found out you grandkids had inherited the place. I decided it was time for a change. I put in my notice at the restaurant. I'm tired of the hustle-bustle there. Thought this place might need a cook. If not, I'll retire."

A cook? Brody leaned back in the chair as he tried on the

idea. "I don't know. Most of us will be living in the cabins. We can probably manage on our own." As he said it, though, the idea of hiring Sonny grew on him. He hated planning and making meals. Felt like a waste of time. Hayden lived on hot dogs and beans, Cooper grilled everything, Seth was too busy to care what he ate, and the girls relied on meal prepping to get through life. "What were you thinking?"

"Breakfast and supper." Sonny spoke with authority. "A warm, hearty breakfast will give you all the energy you need for the day. And I'll get everyone's input on supper options. I'll plan them out a week ahead, do all the shopping, cooking and cleaning up after meals."

Brody almost yelled, "Sold," but refrained. It wasn't his decision to make. And having a chef on site wouldn't come cheap. "What kind of salary are you looking for?"

Sonny told him a ridiculously low figure. "I'd like to live on the ranch again—if you have room. My room and board would be included with that salary."

The ranch had eight cabins—one for Bill, one for Tony, and one for each grandchild. Lillian would be living in his parents' cabin indefinitely, and he couldn't give away Uncle Tony's without permission. But…the lodge itself was empty. And what about the ranch manager's house, available now that the previous manager had moved to Montana?

"All ranch decisions have to be approved by the squad."

"The squad?"

Brody chuckled. "Sorry, that's what I call us. My siblings and cousins—owners of Hudson Ranch, Inc."

Sonny nodded. "I understand."

"I'll call them. If they're on board, the ranch manager's house is empty. We could clean it up for you—"

"The same house down the lane from the stables?" Sonny appeared stricken.

"Yes, why?"

"I grew up in that house."

"Oh, I didn't realize. I should have put two and two together. Is that going to be a problem? We could work out something else."

"It's no problem. None at all. It's why I came. I never expected I might be able to live in my childhood home. God sure has a way of answering prayers sometimes."

"That He does. When I found out Grandpa left us the ranch, I prayed I wasn't the only one who wanted to move here and run it. God answered my prayer."

"I'll be traveling around the area for the next week or so. Here's my number when you've made a decision." Sonny rose, slipped him a business card and shook his hand once more. "It was nice meeting you, Brody."

"Same here. I hope to see you here on a regular basis soon."

"I hope for the same. I'll let myself out."

Brody waited for him to leave, then brought his hands to the back of his head to stretch out his upper back.

Hudson Ranch seemed to be collecting people. First Lillian, now Sonny. And Butch—the dog. Brody hoped everyone would agree to hire Sonny. Would make life easier for all of them. Plus, there was something about the guy Brody was drawn to.

With a deep breath, he surveyed the office. Time to get up to speed on the books before Hayden arrived later tonight. He checked his phone. No texts. No calls. A sliver of disappointment sliced through him.

What had he hoped for? Lillian to check in?

Kind of.

Deep down he knew, though, that asking for help didn't come easily to her. Just as he knew she was probably doing everything she could to find a job right now. He wished she'd relax and let them provide for her for a while. But he doubted her personality would let her. He'd have to keep trying until she trusted him.

Why couldn't a high-paying job she could do from home drop in her lap? Lillian set her phone on the coffee table and stretched her neck from side to side. The cracks and ticks it made didn't sound good. Being at Hudson Ranch for a week had lowered some of her tension, but the uncertainties in her life continued to keep her on high alert.

"Hey, Butch, why don't you go outside for a while? Explore the ranch?" She petted his head as he panted. From the minute the dog arrived on the ranch, he had glued himself to her side. She'd tried to give him freedom to roam, but he preferred to be in the cabin with her and Jonah over being outside with the ranch hands. Although, now that Brody had arrived, the dog might want to hang out with him. "You can stay with me all the time, big guy, but you might like Brody. He's pretty nice." And pretty gorgeous. And generous. And kind. And...

Rebecca's.

She gave the dog another pet. Lillian couldn't afford to confuse Brody's generosity with his feelings. She'd been a charity case throughout her life and knew firsthand the pain involved when she'd falsely started to believe she actually meant something to the families who'd housed her.

Each one of them had eventually turned her out.

All in the past. Sighing, she grabbed her phone. She'd better make the most of Jonah's naptime. She called her old coworker, Gail, who answered on the second ring. "Hey, Gail."

"It's good to hear from you, doll. What are you up to? Did they ever put that slimy rat who robbed you in prison?" Gail had a colorful way of approaching life.

"Um, no. Not yet. They're working on it." Lillian wished they'd hurry up about it.

"They'd better get on it if you ask me."

She privately agreed. "You don't happen to know of any jobs available that I could work at from home, do you?"

"I wish." Gail grunted. "I'd scoop up one of those myself. Can you believe a patient walked in last week with no shirt, no shoes and peanut butter smeared on his forearms? I don't know what he was on, and I don't particularly care. I've got to get into a different field."

Lillian winced. She and Rebecca had lived in an area that had cheap rent and an assortment of characters on the streets. Gail's job was at the hospital about a mile from their old apartment. "If you hear of anything—part-time would be great—would you let me know?"

"Sure, doll. What if something pops up in person?"

"That won't work. I moved out of state."

"Good for you. Get a fresh start."

"I hope so."

"Give that baby a smoosh and kiss from me."

"I will."

Lillian ended the call and stroked Butch's back. The tranquility of Hudson Ranch was a sharp contrast to the life she'd been living. Here, she didn't have to worry about the dangers involved in a rough part of town.

A knock on the door made her jump. Butch didn't bark, simply ambled over to it. Lillian followed, opening it a crack. At the sight of Brody, she grinned and opened it wide.

"Hey, Lil." He bent to pet Butch. "How are you doing today?"

"Great. Come in."

As he stepped inside, his presence made the cabin feel more intimate. Needing some space, she backed up quickly.

"So how's day one going?" She turned to the kitchenette and glanced back over her shoulder. "Want something to drink?"

"Do you have anything hot?" He'd taken off his coat and gloves and was rubbing his hands together.

"Cold out there, huh?" She poured coffee into two mugs and brought one over to Brody, who had taken a seat in the recliner. He smiled his thanks as he took it, and flutters sprang up in her chest.

"The temperature didn't bother me until a few minutes ago. I checked on all the Herefords out in the far pasture. Felt great to be outside again instead of in a cubicle or on the road."

"I forget what your job entailed." She got comfortable on the couch as the ginormous dog settled on the rug with his chin on his paws.

"I was a territory manager for a genomics company that specialized in livestock. When I wasn't traveling for meetings with cattle producers, I was behind a desk selling software to help with herd management, animal monitoring and identification."

"I'm sure you were good at it."

"Number one in the company two years in a row." The pride in his voice made her smile.

"Any regrets about quitting?" She took a sip, keeping an ear open for signs of Jonah waking up.

"No. I'm dumbfounded I actually have the opportunity to run this place—with everyone else, of course. I've always wanted to be my own boss. Use the products I was selling. And now I have the chance."

"You'll be terrific."

"You think so?" It was the first tear in his confidence she'd seen.

"Of course. You're unstoppable."

He seemed to consider it. "I hope you're right."

What would it be like to have some of that unstoppableness herself? She wouldn't know. She'd been at sea for years and years. Every time she'd thought she was getting somewhere the boat would leak and she'd have to jump ship. Tread water.

It hadn't been so bad. She'd always had Rebecca. But now...

"We had a visitor today." Brody had a contented air about him. Lillian hadn't seen any vehicles drive in, but then, the cabins were tucked on a private circular drive down from the lodge and far away from the outbuildings. "He grew up here. Wants to be our chef."

A chef? Sounded fancy. And expensive. And wonderful.

"What did you tell him?" She could stare into Brody's brown eyes all day.

"I told him I'd have to run it by the squad."

"Is hiring him even a possibility?"

He nodded. "I think so. He's not asking for much pay. He'd stay in the old manager's house—he grew up in it, if you can believe that. Now that it's empty, we have the room for him."

A chef. A ranch. A bajillion acres of Wyoming land.

Lillian's skin prickled. She'd better get serious about finding a job. A girl could get comfortable here, and that would only lead to devastation when they decided she had to leave.

Another knock sounded. She scrambled to her feet and hurried to the door. Meena stood there, and Lillian urged her inside. She really liked Brody's energetic sister.

"Oh, good, you're here, too." Meena shivered as she stepped into the living area, and Brody rose, mug in hand. "I've got to leave. My dumb job wants me there all week for presentations."

Meena worked remotely for a home interior design company and took it personally when they required her to work in person.

"You need a ride to the airport?" Brody had the confident stance of a man in charge.

"No, I'm packing light and will drive there in a few hours. But first, I wanted to run something by Lil."

"Am I allowed to stay, or is this a girls-only conversation?" He looked put-out at the thought.

"You can stay. It's about the Christmas market."

"What Christmas market?" Brody asked.

"Fairwood's Christmas market." Meena widened her eyes and gave him a look that screamed *duh*. "It's the first weekend in December. I signed up for a booth."

"Why would you do that?" His face scrunched.

"Because I'm selling crafts." She opened her palms and scoffed. "Obviously."

"What crafts?" he asked.

"That's the problem." Meena turned to Lillian. "What can I make in a hurry to sell?"

"Don't ask me." Lillian backed up a step. She'd never been crafty.

"But you have good ideas." Meena had her pleading face on. "Think."

Lillian glanced at Butch on the rug. "I don't know. What were you making for Seth's cabin?"

"The dog houses that fit over the crates?"

"No, the twisty thing for the candle."

Meena's face brightened. "Yes. I could make wreaths!"

Brody shook his head dramatically. "Wreaths? How did you get wreath out of a twisty candle?"

"Never you mind." She held her palm out to him and addressed Lillian. "Scratch that. It's too ambitious this late in the game. What else have you got?"

Her church in Omaha came to mind. "The church I attended used to put on an Advent event for kids. The children enjoyed making ornaments to take home. They listened to Bible stories and decorated cookies."

"That's it." Meena got the faraway gleam in her eye Lillian was coming to recognize as her idea face. "Ornament kits for children. We'll put together little packages for different ages. You're a genius, Lil! I'm going to need another set of hands to put the kits together. Will twenty bucks an hour be enough for you?"

Lillian stared at Meena, then Brody, then Meena again. Was his sister talking to her?

"I'm confused." Lillian stared at her lukewarm coffee. Any money coming in would be a dream come true, but this family had already given her too much.

"I'm selling ornament kits for children at the Christmas market, and I need help assembling them. I'll pay you twenty dollars an hour. Are you in?"

"I'll help you put the kits together for free." Lillian set the mug on the counter before giving Meena her full attention.

"Nope. I'm paying you. I plan on making a profit, you know, so it would only be fair." The beauty's blue eyes and heart-shaped face were impossible to say no to.

"Yes, but we're friends."

"And friends don't take advantage of each other." Meena gave her a firm nod. "Good. Now that we have that settled."

"All I've done is take advantage of you." Lillian looked from her to Brody. "You guys gave me a home, food, baby supplies. I want to give something back."

"Don't be silly. You're not taking advantage of anything. I have to hire someone, and it might as well be you. I prefer you, to be honest. I don't have the energy for one of the local teens. All that small talk and slang I'm not familiar with. A kid yelled 'skibidi' to me the other day. What does that even mean?"

"I'm not the person to ask," Lillian assured her.

"This is going to be fun. And Jonah can join us." Meena turned to Brody. "I'm going to need long tables set up in the pole barn where Grandma and Grandpa had parties. It's still heated, right?"

"It should be. I'll check on it." Brody went to the kitchenette and set his mug in the sink. "Lil, do you think Butch would want to head over to the pole barn with me?"

"I hope so. I feel bad he's in here with me all the time. It would do him good to stretch his legs around the ranch."

"Okay, I'll check on the pole barn and bring Butch back later. Hayden will be arriving after supper."

"I'll be gone before then." Meena shrugged.

"I'll be here with Jonah."

Brody put his coat back on. "Why don't you bring Jonah to the lodge for supper? I'll get a fire going. That way you can stretch your legs a bit, too."

Lillian should say no. But it would be nice to leave the cabin. Besides, she'd made Brody a promise, and he'd yet to cash in. Maybe he wanted some of those questions answered.

She'd better start preparing what she was going to tell him. Didn't want to get caught off guard and accidentally paint Rebecca in a bad light. The sharp pain in her chest warned her the conversation wouldn't be easy. But, then, what in her life ever was?

"What time should I come over?" A promise was a promise.

"How about six?"

"I'll be there." It would be good to get it over with. Answer his questions. Move on with her life. But she couldn't move on with her life at Hudson Ranch. This was merely an oasis, a place to rest and regroup. Then she'd be on her own again, and this time she wouldn't have Rebecca to rely on, only herself. Maybe it was better that way. She supposed she was going to find out.

Chapter Five

Brody stoked the fire in the lodge's fireplace a few minutes before six. He'd been anticipating sharing tonight's meal with Lillian ever since she'd agreed earlier. She'd declined his offer to pick her up, texting him she was looking forward to the short stroll with the baby. He'd put together a simple meal of spaghetti and meatballs—frozen from the store—and a salad. While he could have eaten alone, he'd wanted to share the satisfaction of his first full day on the ranch with someone, and Lillian had the peaceful presence he craved.

Two knocks preceded the front door opening. He hurried across the room to help her get the stroller inside.

"Here, let me." He unstrapped Jonah and lifted him out, surprised at how light the tiny fellow was even in his fleece outerwear. The hood had little ears. Cute. After Lillian had taken off her coat and shoes, she picked up the diaper bag and reached for the baby. Brody shook his head. "I can hold him for now if you'd like."

She nodded shyly. "Just let me get this off so he doesn't overheat."

Lillian made quick work of getting him out of the fleece one-piece. She kissed his nose, and her tender smile stole Brody's breath. Her beauty had been creeping up on him. And her affection for the child did something funny to his heart.

He cradled the baby in the crook of his arm and headed to the kitchen. The table was set for two. Lillian unsnapped the infant seat from the stroller and carried it to the floor next to one of the chairs.

"Do you need to heat up a bottle or anything?" Brody handed her the baby, then went to the stove and began plating their food.

"No, I fed him before coming over." She was making silly faces, and Jonah's little hands and feet pumped with excitement.

"He's happy. Is he always like this?"

"Mostly. He gets crabby after he wakes up from his afternoon nap. And he cries when he's hungry or needs a diaper change. I've gotten much better at anticipating his needs."

Brody came over and set their plates on the table. "Want anything to drink?"

"A glass of water, please."

He made quick work of pouring two glasses. Then he sat across from her. "Should we pray?"

Her quick nod was enough. Brody said a table prayer, and they both dug into the spaghetti.

"What have you been up to all week?" He twirled his fork in the noodles.

"I made a lot of calls, applied for several jobs and researched baby development. I'm getting used to Jonah's schedule. At least I hope I am. It could change tomorrow. I have no idea."

"You're doing great."

She shook her head and let out a half laugh, half snort. "Hardly."

"What do you mean? You've never been a mom, and you're a natural."

"I don't feel like a natural. I feel like a fake."

He set his fork down and stared at her until she met his gaze. "There's nothing fake about you, Lil."

Her surprised expression made him frown. Didn't anyone ever compliment her? "How did the calls go?" Part of him hoped she wouldn't find a job soon, but it was unrealistic on his part.

"Okay, I guess. I contacted everyone I knew to keep me posted on jobs I can do from home."

"Didn't we tell you not to worry about that?" He sounded too gruff. He needed to tone it down. "The baby is a full-time job and then some."

"He's my responsibility. I need to support myself." No defensiveness lurked in her tone—just typical, matter-of-fact Lillian.

"You'll work with Meena. On the ornament thing." Did she want to, though? No one had asked her. Meena had basically forced her into it the way his sister tended to do.

"I'd love to help with the kits. But I can't take her money."

"You can and you will." He attempted the stern stare his father used to give him when he didn't bring home all A's on his report card.

She carefully set down her fork. Turned those big blue eyes to him. "Brody, this has to stop."

"What?"

"The charity. It's too much. I can't accept it all."

Right. He should have been more mindful of her pride.

"We don't think of it as charity. We like you. We consider it helping a friend."

She patted a napkin to her lips. "I haven't been your friend in ten years. And I didn't treat you like a friend back then."

So, they were getting into it. Here. Now. On his first day back. During the dinner he'd wanted to relax and enjoy. "That's in the past."

"And festering in the present."

He didn't have a response. In his mind, he'd cut Rebecca out of the equation. She'd died. Lillian needed help. End of story.

But she had a point. All those answers he'd longed for had been scaring him lately. That's why he hadn't asked them.

"We don't have to do this," he said.

"What if I told you a little bit about her when she was young?"

"Why?" Shouldn't he be the one pressing for information?

"I have this dread that comes over me." The anxiety in her expression bothered him. "It presses against my chest."

And that's why he wasn't sure he wanted answers anymore. Whatever she dreaded would certainly hurt him.

"I don't know." He hated that he was wimping out on this, but...

"Rebecca and I were intertwined. I wouldn't be me without her. She's part of who I am."

He nudged the plate aside, clenching his jaw. "I'm not ready, Lil. I thought I was, but I'm not."

Why did she look so sad? Probably because he was basically saying he didn't want to know about that part of her. And it clearly was vital. Lillian didn't get it, though. Rebecca had been part of him, too. He'd learned to live without her, hadn't he? She would, as well.

"I won't force it on you." Lillian picked up her fork and pushed the pasta around the plate. "I don't know why I'm pressing this at all. It's hard for me to talk about her. To think about her."

He was being selfish. Her loss was fresh, and his was a decade old. "I guess it couldn't hurt to find out how you met." He could handle that. He hoped.

A pained expression crossed her face. "How much did she tell you about her childhood?"

"Not much. I knew her parents had died, and that's about it."

"Before I say another word, you have to understand something. Rebecca never lied to hurt people. She did it to protect herself."

Brody stiffened. Lillian was already accusing Rebecca of lying? He wanted to push his chair back, get to his feet and pace. But he didn't. He'd be mature about this.

What exactly had Rebecca lied about?

She took a sip of water and set the glass down. "Did she tell you about the foster homes?"

"Foster homes?"

Lillian nodded, then checked on the baby, who was in his seat, trying to shove his entire fist into his mouth. Brody stifled a smile. The kid was adorable.

"Child services took her away from her mom when she was six. She never knew her dad."

"Her mother's alive?"

"Not anymore. She died a while back." Lillian didn't meet his eyes. "She had mental health issues."

"I had no idea. I thought she'd grown up with both parents, and that they'd died when she was in high school."

"Is that what she told you?" She sounded curious, and her eyes shifted as she processed the information.

He dredged his memories. "Honestly, I don't know. The way she talked... I could have assumed it."

"Even if you'd pressed her for details, I doubt she'd have told you all of them."

He disagreed. He and Rebecca had shared their deepest fears, their hopes, their dreams. She'd have told him anything. Right?

"Rebecca and I met when I was ten years old. She was a few months older than me. I'd been living in a foster home near Kansas City. Lots of kids in that house. Not much supervision. When she arrived, my entire life changed for the better. Even as a little girl, she had sass and sparkle. She stole the spotlight wherever she went. I was so grateful to be her shadow." Lillian had a faraway look of fondness in her eyes.

That sounded like Rebecca. He wished he could have met her as a kid. But he didn't like the way Lillian was describing herself. The woman sitting across from him was nobody's shadow.

"How long had you been at the foster home?"

She jerked her head as if surprised. "Me?"

"Yes. You." Why was she so shocked?

"I thought we were talking about Rebecca."

"Is it a crime to want to know about you, too?"

The way her mouth dropped open made him question things. How many people had taken the time to get to know—really know—Lillian Splendor?

"It's just uncommon."

"What is?" he asked.

"Never mind. To answer your question, I'd been in the foster-care system since I was three."

"What did that look like?" He assumed from her phrasing that she'd been in more than one home.

"I was placed in new homes often. Some lasted a few months, others longer. I lost count of how many I stayed in. Probably six or seven. Maybe more."

He wasn't expecting that. "With different adults in charge?"

"Yes. Different foster parents. Different foster siblings."

"Hot sauce and fire," he said under his breath. "Didn't you have anyone else to rely on? Grandparents? Anyone?"

"No. Not until Rebecca arrived." Her serene smile ripped down his defenses. He was beginning to see why Rebecca had meant so much to her. She'd literally had no one else.

"Did you and Rebecca hit it off right away?"

"Yes. We shared a room. We were instant besties. She told me how much she hated the previous home she'd been in. And I told her to lock the bathroom door at all times, and to never, ever be in the same room alone with Toby."

His heart sank.

"Toby had a lot of problems," she continued. "He tried to corner me more than once, but I was always able to escape. The final time, I kicked him where it counts and told my caseworker about him. He got moved to an all-boys' home soon after."

Thank You, Jesus. Brody exhaled, not sure he could handle whatever else she was about to tell him.

"Rebecca and I lasted a long time at that house. Other kids came and went, but we tried very hard to help the parents so they'd let us stay together."

"Were you ever separated?"

"Unfortunately, yes. The foster family no longer wanted us—or any kids—when we were in high school. So I went to one home, and she went to another. Thankfully, we lived in the same school district and attended the same high school."

While Brody preferred to be kept in the dark about some things, he knew it would eat him alive if he didn't ask.

"Were you or Rebecca abused in any way growing up?" He tried to prepare himself for her answer.

"Yes. We both were."

His composure crumpled as his muscles tightened. No. That wasn't what he'd wanted to hear.

"She was molested for a few months as a child by an older

boy. Thankfully, she was placed with a different family and never dealt with it again."

His heart was breaking. He couldn't handle this. Couldn't bear to think of Rebecca as an innocent little girl being abused by anyone and especially not that way.

"And you?" His voice was raspy. *Not Lillian, too.*

"One foster parent solved every problem with fists." No emotion came through her voice. "I spent six months with bruises all over my body. Not my face, though. Other than that, the only time I fought off sexual advances was with Toby. I'm thankful to have been spared."

Thankful. He rubbed his chin. She shouldn't have had to deal with that. Shouldn't have had to fight off an older boy. Shouldn't have been beaten as a child. What could she possibly be thankful for?

Who'd watched out for her? Why hadn't anyone guarded those little girls?

"How did you and Rebecca stay so positive?" He was thinking back to when they'd first met. They'd been happy. Fun to be around. No one ever would have guessed what they'd been through. He'd never had a clue.

Her shoulders relaxed, and her features softened. "We had each other."

He took a drink of water. His mind struggled to take in everything she was telling him.

"It wasn't all bad, Brody. I remember our first Christmas together. Rebecca and I made each other presents. She asked our foster mom for an old picture frame, and she glued pink sequins all over it for me. I loved it so much, even when all the sequins fell off. And I made her a small book. I drew pictures of us—they were terrible, by the way—I'm no artist— and the things we liked best."

The pain inside leveled out a bit, but he had to know one

more thing. "The abuse you mentioned—for both of you—was that the worst of your childhood? Or was there more?"

Her expression fogged over as she considered. "Before Rebecca arrived, the worst thing for me was being on my own. Even in a foster home, I felt completely alone in the world. I mean, besides my caseworker, I basically was alone in the world. That was the worst. That's why Rebecca was so important to me. We were each other's family. We had no one else."

Brody let it sink in. He couldn't step inside her shoes because he'd always had family. Two parents—admittedly absorbed with their work—siblings, cousins, grandparents. His life had been stable and most of his needs had been met.

But Lillian and Rebecca... They'd had places to live and food on the table, but they'd missed out on stability and the love of parents.

Her expression grew less pinched and more open. He had an all-new appreciation for Lillian. "I'm glad you came here, Lil."

She gave him a sweet smile. "I'm glad I came here, too. Thank you for providing a safe place for me and Jonah."

Those words brought down walls he hadn't known he'd erected. And it got him wondering if he was toying with getting hurt by having her here. He'd been gravitating to her, and she planned on leaving. Just like Rebecca had.

He'd better focus his energy on the ranch. He'd had his heart broken once. And once was enough for a lifetime.

Living in Fairwood was looking better and better. The sun shone brightly the following morning as Lillian carried Jonah in his car seat out of Fairwood Community Church to the parking lot out back. She'd been surprised at how friendly everyone had been. Of course, the ladies loved the baby—

who wouldn't?—and people of all ages made a point to welcome her.

The diaper bag strap fell from her shoulder to her forearm, and she set the baby seat on the blacktop to adjust it. She was pretty sure her arms were getting muscles they'd never had before from lugging the baby around. Soon she made it to her car, locked the seat into the base and settled into the driver's seat.

With free time on her hands, it seemed like the perfect opportunity to explore the town.

She drove the few blocks to Hickory Street, found a parking spot in front of Mane Attraction—a hair salon from the looks of it—and took out the stroller from the trunk. The car seat locked into the stroller—she'd be forever grateful for the modular design—and she tucked a blanket around the baby.

"We're going for a walk, buddy." She crinkled her nose in a smile to him, and—wait, did he smile back? Precious baby! "You smiled, didn't you? Oh, you're so sweet."

How she wished Rebecca could be here to see this.

She began pushing Jonah down the sidewalk, noting the businesses as she walked. The town had been decorated for Christmas with wreaths hanging from lampposts, colorful plaid bows and strings of lights wrapped around trees.

Last night's supper with Brody had been cathartic in many ways. It had given her a chance to help him understand Rebecca's past. She'd been surprised that he'd asked her about her own. People usually didn't. They also accused her of being aloof.

Lillian had never personally thought of herself as being aloof. If she had to label herself, she'd say reserved was the right word. She didn't volunteer information about herself, and she was perfectly content letting other people take center stage.

But Brody had asked, and she'd answered. And she felt bad for hurting him with the truth. He'd looked sucker-punched when she'd told him about the abuse. She and Rebecca had talked to each other openly about their situations. And over time they'd found their own ways to deal with the pain.

Lillian had realized she needed a Savior while Rebecca had self-medicated.

The stroller bumped on a crack in the sidewalk. She gave it a good shove, and they were on their way again.

At least Rebecca had come to faith, too, over the past couple of years. How strong that faith was, Lillian didn't know, but she trusted it had been at least as big as a mustard seed.

"We're treating ourselves today, Jonah-bear." She could look at his cute face all day. Actually, she'd been staring at his cute face all day ever since arriving at Hudson Ranch. The baby had been helping heal her inner wounds. And Brody and Meena had been helping, too.

With her bank account restored, Lillian figured an inexpensive breakfast at Tootsie's Diner wouldn't break her. The striped awning over the entrance to the brick building sheltered customers as they entered and exited. An evergreen garland had been strung over the doorframe, and two skinny artificial Christmas trees with white lights stood on either side of the door. She steered the stroller inside.

The place was hopping. She had to wait ten minutes for a table.

A waitress in a hot-pink T-shirt and jeans stopped by to take her order. Jonah's eyelids were drooping, so she gently rocked the car seat next to her in the booth. After ordering orange juice, two eggs, sausage links and sourdough toast, Lillian let her elbows drop on the paper placemat. The baby had fallen asleep. How anyone could sleep in this noisy diner filled with laughter, loud chatter and the aroma of bacon and coffee she'd never know.

Once the waitress set the orange juice in front of her, her thoughts went to the future. The social security office had already gotten back to her about Jonah's benefits. They would be starting payments in the next week or two.

Tomorrow, she planned on opening a bank account here in Fairwood. Keep her money local and easy to access. With a sip of coffee, she thought about how nice it would be to help Meena with the ornaments for the Christmas market. The Hudsons were all so kind to her. She'd repay them...somehow.

And in the meantime, she'd keep looking for a work-from-home job. As soon as she felt reasonably sure she could provide for Jonah without the Hudsons' help, she'd move into an apartment here in town.

Experience had taught her not to wear out her welcome. With Rebecca gone, she couldn't depend on anyone but herself. She'd have to trust the Lord to provide and do everything in her power to be independent.

Her food arrived, and she savored each bite. This week had given her much-needed rest. Her appetite had returned, and she was finally starting to feel like herself again.

All because of Brody.

It would be as simple as snapping her fingers to fall for the handsome cowboy. In college, he'd been off-limits, and honestly, she'd never allowed herself to view him as anything other than Rebecca's boyfriend. But now?

Now she had to protect her heart. She'd dated here and there over the years, but she'd rarely made it past a third date before ending it. She'd never wanted just any man in her life—she'd wanted the right man in her life.

Could Brody be the right man?

No. She shook her head slightly, not caring she was out in

public. Rebecca might be gone, but Brody was still off-limits. He'd never have the depth of feelings for Lillian that he had for Rebecca. And she wouldn't live a life of being second-best.

Better to be alone. She was used to it.

Fifteen minutes later, she'd paid her bill and pushed the stroller with Jonah still asleep down Hickory Street to the park up ahead with the gazebo. As she passed by, she noted the pavilion and playground. If all went well, next year she'd be swinging Jonah in one of those baby swings. And the next? Chasing him around, catching him as he came down the slide. The thought made her steps light.

She returned to the car and drove down the side streets—most of them had names of trees—Maple Street, Evergreen Lane, Oak Drive. Tidy, well-kept bungalows and older homes with small lawns abounded. Maybe someday she'd be able to afford a house of her own with a yard for Jonah to play in. Wouldn't that be something?

As she drove back to the ranch, she realized how much easier it would be to save money with Rebecca out of the picture. They'd shared expenses, and Lillian had resented the many times Rebecca had splurged on something without discussing it first. She'd known her friend had kept a stash of money for herself—the drugs she'd been taking hadn't come cheap. More often than not, Lillian's income had paid their bills, leaving her very little to set aside for a rainy day.

She gripped the steering wheel, forcing the thoughts away to focus instead on the wheat-colored grass of the prairies on either side of the road. Rebecca hadn't been perfect, and neither had Lillian. She'd wanted Rebecca to handle life better. They'd argued about it occasionally, and Rebecca would yell at her to mind her own business. All too often, she'd felt responsible for her friend.

Why was she thinking about this? They'd had a great relationship. Those issues were minor.

She turned into the driveway under the Hudson Ranch sign and marveled at the beautiful land spread out before her. Cattle grazed in the distance, and she drove past the lodge to where the cabins were located. She parked in front of hers and was in the process of taking Jonah's seat out from the back when a voice surprised her.

"Can I help?"

She glanced over her shoulder and smiled. Hayden had arrived. "No thanks. I've got it."

"Are you sure? Looks heavy." He touched the brim of his Stetson and frowned.

"He's still little, so it's not too bad."

"What else you got in there? Anything I can carry?"

"Just my diaper bag, and I can handle it." She hoisted the car seat as Hayden shut the car door. He held out his hand for the carrier, and she gave it to him, figuring he wouldn't be satisfied unless he was helping. "When did you arrive?"

"Late last night. Brody and I spent all morning riding around the ranch." He had a pensive air about him as he walked beside her to the porch steps of her cabin. Butch was lying on the welcome mat, and he brought his head up, tail wagging, as they approached.

"Hey, there, Butchie." She bent to pet him.

"When did you get a dog?" Hayden let Butch smell the back of one hand as he kept a firm grip on the car seat's handle with the other.

"He's not technically mine. He kind of made the ranch his home." The same as she had. "Is everything okay?"

He shrugged. "We've got some repairs to make. Some upgrades are needed, too."

"I'm sure you and Brody will get right on it." She dug through her purse to find the key.

"Yeah." He didn't sound excited.

"Is there something standing in the way of making the repairs?"

"No." He waited for her to unlock the door, then held it open for her. "I want to make sure we're doing the right thing. My cousin and I are not always on the same page."

Boy, could she relate to that. She and Rebecca had been at odds with each other, especially this past year. She stopped short. This was the second time today she'd been thinking about their differences. A lot of them revolved around money and life choices. Before now, she'd never thought about it much.

Maybe I never allowed myself to think about it. Financial decisions had always been Rebecca's way or the highway.

Now she really did feel disloyal.

Lillian set the diaper bag on the floor. Jonah was still sleeping. He could nap in his cozy car seat a while longer.

"Do you want a cup of tea or coffee?" She trucked her thumb toward the kitchenette.

"No. I don't want to bother you." He backed up a step toward the door.

"You're not bothering me. I... I understand what it's like when you're close to someone who has different ideas on how things should be done. Those decisions affect you, too."

"Oh, yeah?" His hazel eyes held questions. "How did you handle it?"

That was a loaded question at the moment. Maybe that's why the topic was on her mind. She didn't want to be in that position again.

"I didn't handle it great." She wrapped her arms around her waist. "I probably should have been more assertive. I was afraid of losing our friendship, so I made compromises I shouldn't have."

"Sounds like you have regrets." His head tilted slightly as he watched her.

Did she? Not really.

"I wouldn't say regrets. More like lessons learned."

He nodded thoughtfully. "I get that. You'd do things differently now."

"Exactly."

"Thanks."

She nodded, doubting she'd helped much, but at least someone wanted her opinion.

"I'll see you around." He tipped his hat and let himself out.

If Lillian kept getting closer to Brody, would she end up compromising again? Too much? The way she had with Rebecca?

Just another reason she needed to find a job and get her own place. As much as she enjoyed being here, she'd never be one of them. She'd have to trust God to open up a job opportunity when the time was right. And she hoped the time would be right soon. That way she wouldn't have to worry about falling for her best friend's ex.

Chapter Six

"A situation came up." Monday evening, Brody and Hayden were staring at Brody's laptop, and from boxes on the screen, Seth, Cooper, Kylie and Meena stared back at them. Brody had wanted to talk to them over the weekend, but no one had been available for a video call until now. "Do any of you remember Grandpa talking about Jeff Armstrong?"

"Grandpa's best friend," Cooper said. "His right-hand man for years."

Brody was surprised Cooper remembered. "Correct. Jeff's son, Sonny Armstrong, stopped by last weekend. He grew up here. Wants to get back to his roots, I guess, and he'd like to live here and be our chef."

"A chef?" Kylie sounded excited.

"Does he have any experience?" Seth looked confused.

"Who cares?" Kylie practically yelled. "If I don't have to cook, I'm all for it."

"Same here." Meena gave them a thumbs-up.

Brody raised his hand. "He's been an executive chef for restaurants all over the world—"

"How much is this going to cost us?" Cooper narrowed his eyes.

Brody told them the salary and quickly added, "He'll be

staying in the ranch manager's house. He'd be cooking breakfasts and suppers for us."

"He'll need a day or two off." Leave it to Seth to be pragmatic. "We don't want to work him to death."

"Yeah, if he's a good cook, we need to make sure he stays," Meena said. "Do we know if he's a good cook?"

"I'll ask him to come over and make a meal," Brody said. "Hayden and I will test it."

"And Lillian," Meena said. "Make sure she tries the food if I'm not back in time."

Brody didn't argue. He respected Lillian's opinion.

"Hayden, what do you think? Is this a good idea?" Kylie asked. She tended to refer to her brothers for guidance.

Brody ground his teeth together and kept his mouth shut. He and Hayden hadn't exactly seen eye to eye since his cousin had arrived. Hayden had already downplayed every one of Brody's suggestions for the ranch, and he'd only been there a few days.

"I think a friend of Grandpa's is a friend of ours," Hayden said. "It would be a blessing for us to not have to worry about meals."

Brody blinked in surprise. Hayden actually approved of spending money? On a nonessential?

"Let's have a vote," he said before Hayden could change his mind. "All in favor, raise your hand."

Six hands shot up. He grinned. "Looks like we have a chef. I'll call Sonny. Don't worry—we'll sample his food before telling him the good news."

"Do you think he can start working before Thanksgiving?" Kylie tapped a finger against her lips. "None of us are qualified to make a turkey."

"We can't make the man work on Thanksgiving, Kylie." Meena rolled her eyes. "I'm sure he has a family. Brody—"

Meena waited until she got his attention "—you have to go over to the ranch manager house and clean it up. Take pictures. I'll add it to the remodeling list."

"Haven't we spent enough on remodeling projects?" Hayden sighed.

"No, we haven't." Meena pursed her lips. "I'm under budget for every cabin. And remember Grandpa's motto? 'An ounce of prevention is worth a pound of cure.'"

"Ben Franklin said that," Cooper said.

"Well, Grandpa did, too." Meena's chin bobbed with attitude.

"Fine." Hayden sounded resigned.

They all caught up for a few more minutes before ending the call. Then Brody turned to Hayden. "I'm glad you agreed about Sonny."

"I'm getting tired of hot dogs and beans." The corner of his mouth lifted in a smile.

Brody clapped his hand on Hayden's shoulder. "So am I, man. So am I. I'm going to run over to the manager's house and see what it needs."

"I'm heading to my cabin. I have the past five years of ledgers to review."

"Don't bother with that now." Brody waved in dismissal. "When I get the herd management software installed, we'll enter all the data. The program will analyze everything we need."

"The software's expensive, Brody."

"I know, but it's worth it." He bristled. "You act like I didn't sell this software for the past five years."

Hayden lifted his gaze to the ceiling. "I don't want to get bulldozed into making these decisions."

"What are you talking about?" He closed the laptop and tucked it under his arm. "Bulldozed?"

"Lillian made a good point—"

"Lillian?" Brody stilled as an uncomfortable sensation filled him. "What does she have to do with this?"

"Nothing. I ran into her yesterday, and she helped me pinpoint something that was bothering me."

"Like what?" He didn't know what he was feeling, but he didn't like it. Lillian was having heart-to-hearts with Hayden? Giving him advice? Behind his back?

"She mentioned making compromises she shouldn't have made out of fear. I want you and I to be honest with each other even when we disagree. Especially when we disagree. This ranch depends on us."

"What compromises did she make?" He hadn't spoken to Lillian yesterday, but their conversation from Saturday night had stuck with him. He found himself curious about her life, her past, who she'd been, who she was. And it bugged him that Hayden knew something he didn't.

He shrugged. "She didn't say. I only know I don't want my relationship with you to sour. I want you to actually listen to my concerns."

Brody almost blurted out a reply, but Hayden's tone stopped him. He studied his cousin. Taller than him, more lanky—and as honest as they came. Maybe he should be more accommodating to his new business partner.

"Point taken." He ran his free hand over his hair. "You're my best friend, and we need to work together to make this ranch a success."

"How do we make big decisions? I appreciate your enthusiasm. I'm just…"

"Realistic." Brody began walking to the front hall. "I guess we do need to figure out a way to make decisions that are fair to both of us."

"What do you have in mind?" Hayden followed him.

He handed Hayden the laptop and put his coat on, then took it back while Hayden zipped up. They went outside and locked the door behind them.

"We'll figure out something."

With a backward wave, Hayden continued toward the lane where the cabins were located, while Brody headed in the opposite direction. Then he realized he still had the laptop. Better drop it off at his cabin first. He loped down the lane and stopped as Butch ambled from Lillian's porch and headed his way.

"Hey, Butch, it's cold out here for you even with all that fur." He ruffled the back of the dog's neck. "Lillian won't let you inside?"

That wasn't like her. She had a soft spot for the big dog. He strode to her cabin and knocked. Crying from the baby came through the door. The hair on the back of his neck rose, and he knocked again.

Lillian opened it. She held Jonah up to her shoulder. Her hair was rumpled, and bags of worry drooped under her eyes. She let him inside, turning to bounce the baby as she murmured shushing sounds.

"What's wrong with Jonah?" He closed the door and followed her into the living area. She stood in front of the couch, gently bouncing the babe, but the cries only got louder.

"I don't know. He won't eat. He doesn't need a diaper change. And he won't stop crying."

He stepped toward her. "Let me hold him. Take a break."

She flashed him a skeptical glance but allowed him to take the baby. Jonah's red face wrinkled as he gazed up at Brody, and a fresh batch of wailing commenced.

Lillian wiped a finger over her eyebrow. "I don't know what to do."

Brody tensed with each cry. *Think. Is the baby in pain? What could be wrong?*

He knew next to nothing about children. However, he knew a lot about cattle. What distressed a baby calf?

Not being near its mama, for one. Being sick, for another.

"Have you taken his temp?" Brody tucked the boy in the crook of his arm, jiggling him to calm him down.

"No. Should I?" Those baby blues held a faint spark of hope.

"I would. He might not feel good." A sense of calm came over him. The baby's cries grew louder. He kept a firm grip on the child and purposely rocked the boy slowly, gently. Lillian disappeared down the hallway to the bedrooms. A few moments later, she returned holding a digital thermometer.

"Let me try under his armpit." While she leaned in to unsnap the outfit, he caught a whiff of her tropical body spray. Wanted to tuck her hair behind her ear. Kiss her cheek. Make her worries go away.

This attraction didn't make sense. This was Lillian. Rebecca's best friend. And he was holding the baby of the woman who'd broken his heart. Everything about it was logically wrong.

"There. I think I got it." The beep had her pulling the thermometer out. "One hundred and one. That's high."

He wanted to run his palm down her arm, reassure her with physical touch. But he didn't. Couldn't.

"It's high, but it's not dangerous." At least he hoped it wasn't. "Do you have any children's ibuprofen?"

"No. The doctors don't recommend it until the baby is older." She nibbled her lower lip, anxiety plastered all over her pretty face. Then she glanced up at him. "What do I do?"

"He's simmering to a whimper." Brody tried to reassure

her. "Maybe he'll fall asleep. His body will fight off whatever's going on."

"What if it doesn't? What if his fever keeps getting higher? What if—" She covered her mouth and turned away.

He set his free hand on her shoulder. "Hey, let's not go to worst-case scenarios. Babies get sick sometimes. God made Jonah's little body strong, and we'll pray he gets better quickly. I'll be right here. I won't leave you."

"Worst-case scenarios are all I know, Brody." The words came out barely above a whisper. He shifted his jaw. From what she'd told him—all she'd been through as a child and recently with Rebecca—she had good reason to say it.

"Let's change that." He shouldn't promise her things outside his control, but he wanted to give her hope. Wasn't God the God of hope? "I'll call Kylie right now. She's a nursing assistant. She'll know what to do. And first thing tomorrow, we'll call the medical clinic in town for an appointment."

The way her eyelashes were fluttering, he'd say she was fighting back tears.

"Thank you," she whispered. Then she pivoted and hurried back down the hall.

He stared down at the baby, almost asleep but still letting out the occasional whimper, and felt a burst of affection for the rosy-cheeked boy.

Jonah would never know his mother. And Rebecca would never see her son grow up.

But Lillian...she'd raise him with love. She'd make sure he knew all about his vibrant mother. Was it fair Lillian had been left to pick up all the shattered pieces from Rebecca's choices, though?

More than ever, he realized how selfless Lillian was being. How blessed he'd been throughout his life. He'd had everything that mattered, and she'd had none of it. No stable home.

No loving parents, grandparents, siblings, cousins. No financial help. No guidance. She'd only had Rebecca. And her best friend was gone.

He wouldn't let Lillian go through life alone, depending only on herself. The Hudsons would be the family she needed. But he'd have to be careful, too. He'd already gotten burned by one woman he'd thought he'd known inside and out. Lillian was a temptation, and she didn't even know it.

Brody couldn't trust her to not cut him out of her life without a warning, and the way Lillian had grown up, he doubted she'd be able to trust him much, either.

He'd better keep telling himself that, or they'd both end up hurt.

He'd stayed. For hours. Holding the baby, reassuring Lillian with his presence.

She should have known he would.

Brody Hudson was too good to be true.

He was also too good for her.

Jonah's fever had broken Tuesday morning, but she'd taken him to the clinic to be sure he was okay. The staff had been kind and helpful. The poor babe had an ear infection. She was thankful to have a doctor nearby. And as the week wore on, the baby returned to his happy, gurgly self.

She couldn't believe it was Saturday, already. Lillian crouched to strap Jonah in the infant seat. She blew kisses to him as she tucked a blanket around his body. Then she took him and the diaper bag outside with Butch next to her and pulled the stroller out of the trunk. She locked the seat into it and pushed Jonah down the lane on her way to the pole barn beyond the ranch buildings. Meena had arrived last night, and Lillian had promised to help get started on the ornament kits this morning.

The clear Wyoming air refreshed her as did the sight of pronghorns running in the distance. The ranch was like something out of a children's picture book. She'd made a habit of watching the sunset each day, marveling at the peach, purple and pink majesty.

She felt safe here. Utterly safe. On Monday, before Jonah got sick, she'd set up a bank account in Fairwood. The first social security check had already been deposited in it, and she'd applied for eight more part-time jobs she could do from home. Six of them were in the medical field, and the other two were with insurance companies.

Yesterday, she'd gotten another call from an attorney working for the prosecuting team. While she was relieved that Benny was still in jail, she didn't know how long it would last. If the case went to trial and he was acquitted, would he come after her? She didn't know. One more thing to continue praying for—God's protection.

The cold began to seep in, and she shivered. Butch trotted ahead of her, and occasionally the stroller hit a rut in the gravel. Up ahead and to the right, an older man was hauling boxes out of the back of an SUV near the door to the mudroom of the lodge.

"Hello," she called. Must be the cook the Hudsons were thinking of hiring. Brody had said the man would be back in Fairwood this weekend.

He glanced up, straightening. "Hello yourself. I'm Sonny Armstrong."

She pushed the stroller his way and stopped a few feet from him. "Lillian Splendor."

"It's a pleasure to meet you, Ms. Splendor. Lovely name you've got."

She was sure she was blushing at his cultured tone. "Thank you. But please, call me Lillian."

"Then you must call me Sonny." His receding salt-and-pepper hair was kept trimmed, and his brown eyes crinkled in the corners. His casual yet fitted clothing hinted at wealth. All in all, he projected an elegant kindness. She liked him instantly.

"Are you here to cook?" she asked.

"Yes. I'm preparing a sampler. If it goes well, I'll be moving to the ranch."

"I hope it goes well. Everyone's excited for you to be here."

"They are?" He turned to take another box from the SUV.

"Yes, I don't think the Hudsons are big on cooking," she said, wanting him to feel comfortable. "They know how blessed they are to hire a professional chef."

"Well, I'll do my best to make sure everyone is fed and happy."

"Fed, yes. Happy?" She shrugged.

"I suppose you're right. Happiness can be an elusive goal."

They exchanged an understanding look, then Lillian nodded to the baby. "I'd better get him out of the cold. I'm looking forward to seeing more of you."

"You, too." He gave her a slight bow, and she continued on her way.

The pole barn came into view. Meena opened the door, thrusting her foot out to keep it from closing, and picked up one of the boxes stacked there before disappearing inside. Looked like Meena had her work cut out for her.

"Oh, hey, you made it." Meena rushed to Lillian and gave her a big hug, then turned to greet the baby. "Is it possible he grew in one week? Look at those chubby cheeks."

"I know. Every day he gets stronger, too. I'm glad he's not sick anymore."

"Here, let's get him inside." Meena opened the door wide while Lillian pushed the stroller over the threshold.

Lillian hadn't been in the pole barn before, and she was

surprised to see linoleum floors and wood paneling on the walls along with a drop ceiling. While not massive, the space could easily accommodate at least fifty people. Long tables butted up end to end had been set up in two rows. Folding chairs were tucked against them.

"I'm almost done getting everything inside. Give me a sec." Meena held up her finger, then went back outside.

Jonah began to fuss, so Lillian took off her coat and got the front-facing baby carrier ready. She found he liked being snuggled up to her more than being left to his own devices between naps. Whenever he slept, she took the opportunity to research—job openings, possible apartments in town, how to raise babies.

She'd been spending a lot of time on the parenting sites—had been learning more about infant development and what he needed. But all the advice sometimes left her confused. She supposed she'd have to trust her instincts.

"Okay, this is it." Meena strode past her with another box and set it beside the others on one of the tables. "I hope I didn't forget to order anything."

From what Lillian could tell, Meena wasn't the type to forget anything.

"Let's open all the boxes and sort the stuff into three groups. I'm making ornament kits for preschoolers, five-to-eight-year-olds and nine-to-twelve-year-olds. Oh, I left my notes on the counter."

Lillian finished getting Jonah settled in the carrier and turned to track where Meena went. A long counter along the far side of the space revealed a kitchen beyond it. Meena waved a stack of papers, beaming as she hurried back to Lillian.

"Here we go." She held up the sheet for the preschool ornament. "I made lists for each kit, and I printed out instructions for the kids to assemble them." She handed Lillian the sheet and described what to do.

Lillian listened, caressing Jonah's wispy hair, as Meena explained how each kit would work.

"I'm amazed you came up with all this on such short notice."

Meena waved in dismissal. "It's nothing. I love crafts. Always have. When I heard about the market, I knew I had to get involved."

"Why don't you open the boxes, and I'll start sorting everything? I don't want to hold a sharp object with the baby right here."

Meena laughed. "No sharp objects for you. I'll get started."

Over the next hour, they moved items to three tables and discussed Meena's job. She found it uninspiring that her days consisted of video calls with clients who needed design advice. While she liked talking to customers, she loved the hands-on work of actually making the ideas come to life, and her current position didn't allow it. They also discussed Lillian's job hunt and how thankful she was the social security benefits had kicked in.

Two hours later, Lillian was warming a bottle in the pole barn's kitchen when her phone rang. Her stomach clenched at the unknown caller from Omaha. Experience told her it had to do with the investigation.

"Hello?"

"Lillian Splendor?"

"Yes."

"This is Yarah Slate. I'm a prosecutor working on Benny Tatter's case. I have a few questions."

Lillian inhaled through her nose and closed her eyes momentarily. The memory of finding Rebecca's dead body slammed into her. How still she'd been. How obvious all her precious life had already drained away. Following the ambulance to the hospital. Then bringing home the baby to chaos. Broken furniture, so many things stolen.

Still in the baby carrier, Jonah kicked his legs and fussed more loudly. He was getting hungry.

"I've given statements. More than once. I don't have anything more to add." She wished the case would go away. Wished she didn't have to be involved at all. Wished she'd never have to think about that night again.

"I understand, and we appreciate your patience. This will only take a few minutes."

A massive bout of heartburn was incoming. If she got this over with, maybe they'd leave her alone.

She'd told herself that the last time. And the time before that.

"Fine. But can you tell me if you have a court date yet?"

"The case hasn't advanced to that stage."

Would it ever advance to that stage? Lillian answered her questions as quickly and thoroughly as possible. When the call ended, she took the baby out of the carrier and shifted him in her arms to feed him. His little gulps took away some of her tension.

Voices from the work area made her wander back out there. Brody and Hayden were talking to Meena.

Brody glanced over and grinned. "Good. You're here, too. Come on over to the lodge. Sonny has a meal for us." He rubbed his hands together, and his childlike glee chased away her worries. "I'll take him so you can get your coat on."

As she drew near, he took the baby from her and gave him the bottle. Brody's winter jacket was unzipped, revealing a sweatshirt, jeans with a large belt buckle and cowboy boots. His face was flushed from the cold.

Lillian found her coat, got Jonah's stuff together and reached for the baby.

"I don't mind carrying him." Brody's gaze ran over her with appreciation. "Ready?"

"Wrap him in this blanket first." They bundled up the baby, and Hayden and Meena, deep in conversation, led the way outside. Lillian pushed the empty stroller.

"What's wrong?" Brody glanced her way as he protected Jonah from the wind.

Should she tell him about the call? Or was she relying on him too much? She depended on him for her home. She shouldn't need his emotional support, too.

"Is it money?" he asked.

"No. I was telling Meena—Jonah's benefits have kicked in already. I just got off the phone with a lawyer working on Benny's case."

Brody slowed. "Did you learn anything?"

"No. They asked the same questions. I've answered them over and over. Why can't they leave me alone?" Her voice caught at the end.

"They're trying to get him prosecuted. Hang in there. You're here with us now. We aren't going to let anything happen to you."

Lillian turned her attention to her hands on the stroller handle. As much as she wanted to believe him, she couldn't. Because he'd emphasized *now*, reminding her she wouldn't be with them forever.

They didn't need her.

But she sure did need them.

And she'd get hurt if she didn't prioritize moving to town. As soon as she landed a job, she'd make plans to leave the ranch. This oasis couldn't last, and she knew it.

Chapter Seven

Sonny Armstrong was a blessing from God.

Lillian set large dinner plates around the long table in the dining room at the lodge Thanksgiving afternoon. Jonah was taking a late afternoon nap in his bouncy seat nearby. It had been less than two weeks since she, Meena, Brody and Hayden had eaten one of the best meals she could remember, and Brody had offered Sonny the job on the spot. The kind man had moved into the former ranch manager's house the following day and insisted on cooking for them ever since. Lillian liked to stick around to help Sonny clean up after breakfast. She enjoyed talking to him. Butch helped clean, too, by eating every crumb off the floor, and he'd decided Sonny was his new person. The lure of all the property on the ranch was lost on the Bernese mountain dog.

She'd also been enjoying getting to know Meena every day when they assembled the ornament kits. They had over half of them finished with pretty red bows on top of each package.

The squad—as Brody called them—had trickled back to the ranch last night and this morning. Kylie had been the final one to arrive, and she'd promptly gone to her cabin for a nap before the big Thanksgiving supper. Speaking of...it smelled amazing. Sonny had insisted on whipping up a traditional feast with turkey, stuffing, mashed potatoes and gravy, corn casserole, cranberry relish, yams and fresh rolls. All homemade, of course. Then there were the pies—two pumpkin, an apple, a pecan and a French silk.

Lillian had watched him in action—the man clearly loved what he did. Sonny was in his element cooking at the lodge. She'd bonded with him, especially after they'd shared a few painful details about their pasts—she told him about Rebecca and Jonah, and he admitted he had a thirty-one-year-old daughter and two grandsons—none of whom had spoken to Sonny in years. Lillian hadn't pressed him about it, but she sympathized with him.

He and Meena weren't the only ones she was getting closer with—she'd been spending time after supper with Brody every night. They talked about the ranch, their hobbies, places to visit—basically, everything but Rebecca, and she wasn't sure how she felt about that.

Regardless, she hoped this Thanksgiving would be a beautiful memory for all of them for years to come.

When she finished setting the plates, she returned to the butler's pantry for silverware. Sonny had shown her the table settings he'd selected, and Meena, naturally, had taken charge of the table decorations. The flower arrangements were an array of autumn tones, and Meena was finishing making handwritten place cards for each person, including Sonny.

Lillian picked up the tray of silverware and pivoted to exit. Brody stood in the doorway. He wore nice jeans and a sweater. No cowboy hat or boots in sight. He looked awfully handsome with that gleam in his eyes and smile teasing his lips.

"What are you doing?" He motioned two fingers for her to hand him the silverware, and she did.

"Helping Sonny get everything ready." Butch ambled over with his tongue panting. "No, Butch. Out." She pointed to the door, and the dog obeyed, wagging his tail in the direction of the kitchen.

Brody took the silverware to the dining room, and Lillian joined him with the cloth napkins she and Meena had folded earlier. She began placing one on top of each plate.

"You look happy for someone on chore duty." He lined butter knives and spoons on one side of each plate and forks on the other.

"Chore duty?" She snorted. "Hardly. Your grandparents have the most gorgeous sets of dinnerware. I'm enjoying this. It's so fancy."

He shot her an amused smile. "How do you usually celebrate Thanksgiving?"

"Rebecca and I would host a friends-giving with coworkers and people who couldn't make it home or had nowhere else to go. We all chipped in and ordered a ready-made meal from our local supermarket." Good times. "Rebecca always greeted everyone as they arrived. She was so good at making people feel like they were honored guests instead of joining a random meal in a not-great apartment. We all felt like we were at a coronation or something. She had such a gift for making you feel…" Her throat grew tight.

"Special," he murmured.

"Yeah. I miss that. I miss her." She continued placing each napkin on the plates as the memories rained down.

"Question for you," Brody said. "Back in college, when she and I were together, did she really go home and spend Thanksgiving with family?"

Family? What family? "Oh, no. Not even close. We crashed in an apartment with two international students who had nowhere else to go. I think we all split a bucket of KFC. I'd forgotten about that." She hadn't cared what they did or where they went—all that had mattered was spending the holidays with her best friend. Rebecca had probably made up a story to convince Brody she had a place to go for the holidays. "Did she tell you she was going to visit family?"

She stood across the table from Brody. He had a stricken look on his face, and she immediately felt bad. She hadn't meant to cause him pain. "I'm sorry, Brody. I forget sometimes that—never mind. I won't say anything more."

"No, no. It's okay." He nodded as if trying to overcome his hurt. "But why? Why wouldn't she tell me she had no place else to go?"

"She was probably embarrassed. I think we both were. As soon as we turned eighteen, we were literally on our own. We both had part-time jobs at fast-food restaurants, and my caseworker helped us apply for low-income housing. Even that was too expensive for us, so after we graduated from high school, we moved to the university and ended up subleasing a room for the summer."

"You were kicked out of your foster homes before graduating from high school?"

"Yeah." It had never felt fair. Several of the other foster kids they'd known who had aged out had stayed in their foster homes until after graduation. Her family and Rebecca's had needed the space to take in younger kids, ones who came with the financial benefits that expired when she turned eighteen.

"Do you ever talk to your foster family? The one who kicked you out?"

"Oh, no." She'd made peace with that a long time ago. "We didn't stay in touch. But I'm thankful they provided me with a roof over my head, meals and an address. You'd be surprised how hard life is if you don't have a permanent address."

He wiped a hand over his mouth. "And Rebecca? Her experience was similar?"

"Yes." It had bothered Rebecca more than Lillian. "I think

she always hoped that the family would grow attached and offer her a place to come back to for holidays and whatnot. When she had to leave before graduating, it was a real blow."

"Wasn't it for you?"

"Not as much." She shook her head, adjusting a napkin to be centered. "I was realistic."

"Rebecca was never realistic," he said quietly. "Big plans. Big personality. Why would she be embarrassed by not having a place to go for Thanksgiving, though? She couldn't help it. Neither of you could."

"Says the man surrounded by family who inherited a ranch," she said jokingly. "Rebecca created a persona for herself in college. One of a smart orphan attending university on a scholarship. Only we didn't have scholarships. We had Pell Grants and federal loans." And they'd only had those because Lillian had done her research and filled out every online form for them both.

"I don't understand why she lied about it all." If his eyebrows drew any closer, they'd merge.

How could she make him understand?

"In her mind, she was leveling the playing field. She was adamant we'd have a fresh start. Everyone in high school had known we were foster kids. It's hard to fit in when the people you want to fit in with have lives that are so different than your own."

Voices carried from the front hallway, and soon Kylie, Seth and Cooper made their way into the dining room.

Cooper rubbed his hands together. "If everything tastes half as good as it smells, I'm going to need to change into my sweatpants."

Brody looked like he wasn't finished with the topic, but he greeted Cooper anyway. And slowly his pinched expression disappeared. He began boasting about Sonny's cooking, and she took the opportunity to slip out of the room to grab the remaining table settings.

He never brought up Rebecca anymore, and Lillian wasn't sure if that was a good or bad thing. She didn't want to hurt him, but she also wanted him to understand.

Understand what? Rebecca's past? Or yours?

Maybe both.

Meena breezed past, then halted and backed up a step. "Hey, are you all right?"

"Of course," she said brightly, stacking water glasses on a tray. "Why?"

"You had a sad look about you. I have the place cards ready. Want to help me put them on the table?"

"Sure. Let me get the rest of the glasses, and I'll be right there." Lillian took care moving all the glasses to the table, where everyone stood to the side laughing and talking. She and Meena put the final touches to the table.

Sonny popped his head into the dining room and announced the meal was almost ready. Lillian hurried into the kitchen to help him transfer food to serving dishes.

"You should be out there enjoying yourself." His fatherly warmth touched her heart. "Leave me to do this."

"I am enjoying myself." It was true. Helping behind the scenes came more naturally to her than keeping up a conversation. "Let me help."

"If you insist. I appreciate it." He had all the serving dishes lined up on the counter, and as he filled them, she took them to the table.

Brody stopped her on her way back. "You don't have to do that."

"I want to help Sonny."

"Then I will, too."

Before she could tell him it wasn't necessary, he strode into the kitchen and grabbed the next dish Sonny set out. Together they transferred all the food. Then Sonny excused himself to take off his apron and wash his hands.

"Everyone, find your place at the table," Brody announced after Sonny joined them. Instrumental music played through a wireless speaker. Lillian checked on Jonah, still sleeping— sweet darling—and found her spot. Right next to Brody's.

He pulled out the chair for her, and she smiled her thanks. Across the table, Meena's saucy expression and arched eyebrows made Lillian want to laugh and shake her head. His sister wasn't subtle. And Lillian loved her all the more for it.

The room quieted as Brody stood. "The man of the hour. Sonny, this meal wouldn't exist without you. We'd probably be heating up frozen turkey or making sandwiches. Thank you from the bottom of all our hearts."

The man nodded, put his hands over his heart in a slight bow, and took a seat near the end of the table next to Seth.

"Everyone, let's keep the Hudson tradition going," Brody said. "Please join hands." Lillian wasn't sure what the tradition entailed, but she took Brody's hand. Then Brody led them in prayer. "Thank you, God, for bringing us together. For blessing us with this ranch, with new friends and with this delicious meal. Amen."

Brody gave her hand an extra squeeze as the conversations started back up. She added her own silent prayer. *Thank You, Lord Jesus, for bringing me here. I don't deserve to be included with them, but I appreciate it. Your mercies are new every morning.*

She'd enjoy this meal and this family while she had them. If she'd learned anything over the years, it was to remember these bright spots when life got dark. She'd be on her own again soon enough.

***

"A slice of pecan, please." Brody held Jonah as Seth asked him and Lillian what kind of pie they wanted. The baby had woken during the meal, and Brody held him so Lillian could finish eating. Jonah's mouth worked on a pacifier as he stared up at Brody's face. The kid was cute with those chubby cheeks.

"You sure you don't want me to take him?" Lillian sipped decaf coffee from one of his grandmother's fancy cups and saucers.

"He's happy. See?" He nodded to the child, who seemed mesmerized by him.

"He likes you." She took another sip, then craned her neck forward. "Sonny, thank you. That was the best Thanksgiving meal I can remember."

"You're welcome, and that's kind of you to say."

Everyone had been raving about the food since taking their first bites. Brody still couldn't believe the chef worked here. What a blessing. Not having to worry about most of his meals had freed up time and mental space. Plus, he'd been getting to know Sonny better, and he appreciated his nonjudgmental personality.

Brody shifted the baby slightly and shot a sideways glance at Lil. The things she'd shared while they were setting the table kept coming back and bothering him.

Kicked out on her eighteenth birthday. Forced into low-income housing until graduation. Moving to the university early. Figuring out financial aid.

Keeping Rebecca's secrets.

He'd always known Rebecca and Lillian were close. He just hadn't understood the extent of it. Had never guessed the reasons why.

And the questions he was itching to ask remained on the tip of his tongue.

Why had Rebecca decided to drop out of college? When had she decided it? And why hadn't she told him?

Rebecca never should have left him without giving him an explanation.

Another question—this one fresh, not moldy from years of neglect—sprang up. What would Rebecca's life have looked like if Lillian hadn't been by her side for all those years?

While the woman he remembered had been a bright light, she'd also been impulsive. Never on time. Always flitting from one thing to the next. He'd found it exciting—had found *her* exciting. But he'd been a twenty-one-year-old. Practically a kid.

And now? If they'd stayed together, would he have been able to handle that kind of energy? Or would it have worn him out?

He'd spent ten years convincing himself Rebecca was the love of his life and there could be no one else, but lately he was beginning to wonder if that was even true.

"Ten minutes, everyone." Hayden tapped his watch.

Best to get his mind on the present and away from the past. Brody leaned in toward Lillian. "Be prepared. Games are coming."

"What kind of games?"

"I don't know. Each Thanksgiving is different. And I feel like they get worse every year."

"Who picks them?"

"Hayden, Seth and Kylie."

"Why them?"

He shrugged. "It's just the way it's always been."

"Huh. I'm sure whatever they choose will be fine." She set the dainty cup in its saucer and shifted to face him. "Oh, I forgot to tell you. Gail, one of my old coworkers, called yesterday. The hospital she works for has a part-time medical data-entry position available. I already applied."

"What do you mean?" He tensed, unsure what the job entailed. "Would you move?"

"No. It's remote." She looked beautiful, peaceful, content. He should be happy for her. "It's exactly what I'm looking for."

"But..." He almost told her she didn't have to work, that they'd provide for her. But he wasn't being fair. Of course she needed a job. Given what she'd told him about her childhood, she'd never be okay without having an income of her own to rely on.

But it worried him. What if she took the position and decided to move back to Omaha?

"If I get it, I should have enough money to find an apartment after the holidays."

Just what he feared. She wanted to leave.

"You don't have to do that."

"I want to be independent." She spoke slowly as if to a child. "I'm not taking advantage of your generosity a minute longer than necessary."

"What's this I heard about a job?" Kylie sat across from Lillian two seats down.

"I might have a shot at a part-time position I can do from home."

"That's great! I need one of those. Something tells me I can't take care of my elderly patients remotely, though."

"No, I think not." Lillian laughed.

Brody didn't see the humor in any of this. He'd gotten used to having Lillian around. He liked helping with the baby. Liked stopping by the pole barn periodically throughout the day when she and Meena were putting those little packages together. Liked walking her back to her cabin from the lodge after supper and lingering for a while each night.

He liked her. Period.

"Here you go." Seth set a plate in front of him with the pecan pie and a plate with pumpkin pie in front of Lillian.

"Thanks, man."

Lillian sliced her fork into the pumpkin pie. "I've been researching available apartments in Fairwood—"

"Why would you do that?" Meena's face looked as confused as his own surely did.

"Why look for apartments?" She slid the bite into her mouth.

"Yeah. You have a place to live. Don't you like the cabin?" His sister sounded stricken. Maybe Brody should have a talk with her. She'd gotten close to Lillian, too. "I can redecorate it for you. I'll make it exactly what you'd like."

When she finished chewing, Lillian addressed Meena. "I love the cabin the way it is."

"Then... I don't understand."

"It's not about the cabin. It's about..." She stared at the corner of the ceiling before addressing Meena. "Stability."

"Do you think the ranch isn't stable?" Meena asked. "Because Brody and Hayden know what they're doing."

"They're more than qualified." Lillian patted her mouth with a napkin. "But I'm not one of you. I'm not a Hudson. This ranch is for you guys, and I need my own thing."

Brody acknowledged the truth in her words. She did need her own thing. She'd been at the mercy of foster homes her entire childhood. Then she and Rebecca had been bound together. He couldn't blame her for not wanting to be at the mercy of Hudson Ranch.

"Leave it be, Meena." He gave her a quick shake of his head, and she sighed, clearly unhappy.

"Everyone, when you finish your pie, head to the living room." Kylie stood, clapping. "We're about ready."

Lillian pushed her dessert plate back and downed the last of her coffee. "I need to change him."

Brody handed her the baby, then nodded to their cups and dishes. "I'll take care of this."

"You can leave it. I'll clear them when I come back."

"No, I'll take care of it now."

As she headed away with the baby and diaper bag, he rose to clear their plates.

In the past month, he'd gotten everything he'd been wanting for years. He should be shouting his thanks to God on this Thanksgiving. However, all he seemed to be focusing on was his disappointment that Lillian wanted to move on with her life.

Shouldn't he be helping her move on?

Lillian and Rebecca had shared the same upbringings, the same survival stories. Sooner or later Lillian would cut him out of her life the way Rebecca had. And he'd better start preparing for it, or he was going to be crushed.

Chapter Eight

The community center had been transformed into a winter wonderland for the Christmas market. Lillian held Jonah on her hip as she took a break from helping Meena sell the ornament kits. She'd been here all morning, and she craved hot chocolate. It had been over a week since Thanksgiving, and she couldn't stop thinking about all the fun they'd had playing Pictionary, charades and a particularly competitive round of UNO.

The longer she stayed at Hudson Ranch, the more she wanted to live there in her cabin forever.

She'd never been one to indulge in fantasies, though. The Hudsons didn't need her, but she needed them—too much. And that meant she had to get a few inches of separation from Brody and his family.

Coming here had always been a last-ditch, getting-back-on-her-feet move, nothing permanent. Permanence and dreams coming true were for other people, not for her.

"A Holly Jolly Christmas" blared through the speakers as she carried Jonah in the direction of the corner that had a hot cocoa stand. A mix of cinnamon, coffee and evergreen scents drifted in the air as she dodged people. Lillian's heart warmed at the sight of a couple trying to keep hold of their toddler girl's hands. That would be her in a year or two. Trying to keep hold of Jonah.

Male laughter made her glance to her left. Brody and Hayden had arrived and were chatting with two attractive brunettes who appeared to be in their midtwenties. Both women were stunning. Lillian shrank into her navy sweater and faded jeans. This morning she'd pushed her hair back from her face with a headband, dusted her face with powder, swiped mascara on her eyelashes and applied a rose-colored lip gloss. Compared to the women's fresh-faced beauty and formfitting clothing, Lillian could only describe herself as frumpy.

Oh, well. She'd never been a beauty queen.

She was kind of surprised she hadn't noticed Brody or Hayden come in. How long had they been there? And how familiar were they with the women who kept making them laugh?

"My, what a cute little baby you've got there." A full-figured woman with shoulder-length silver hair and a cheerful face stopped her. "What's his name?"

"This is Jonah." She brushed wispy hair away from his forehead, then let him curl his fingers around her pinkie.

"Hi, there, Jonah," the woman cooed, then stared at her. "What's your name, honey?"

"I'm Lillian Splendor." She bounced him lightly.

"Fran Bolenski. Fairwood's been my home for thirty-five years. I live over on Birch Street in the white duplex. I saw you and this scoop of cuteness at church last week, and I got distracted by Jackie—she's secretary of the women's group—before I could introduce myself."

"It's nice to meet you." Lillian stepped forward for people to pass by in the wide aisle between booths.

"If you ever need a sitter, give me a holler. My kids are grown up. They both moved away. Anne has two babies, and

Alex hasn't met the right gal, yet. Say, are you single?" Her light brown eyes blinked with hope.

Lillian swallowed, not wanting to get set up on a blind date. "Yes. But I'm not—"

"Next time he's in town, I'll let you know. You two could grab some supper. Get to know each other."

"Um, I don't know about—"

"If you need a place to stay, the other side of my duplex will be available soon. Then Alex could drop by whenever he's in town."

"Hey, Lil." Brody sidled up next to her, and she instinctively held her breath at his nearness. He tickled Jonah's elbow. "Hi, buddy. Why are you eating your fist?"

"You must be one of those Hudson boys," Fran said. "I remember you. Brady, is it?"

"Close." He held out his hand to her. "Brody Hudson."

"This is Fran Bolenski," Lillian said, glancing up at him. "She lives in town."

"I was telling your friend here about my Alex. Single." Fran unzipped her fanny pack and took out a cell phone. "Here's a picture to help seal the deal. He's good-looking."

Seal what deal? Should Lillian protest or stay silent? Maybe another tactic would work. "Where does Alex live?"

Brody flashed Lillian a frown. What? She was trying to find a way out of this as tactfully as possible.

Fran's index finger swiped through her phone as she focused on the screen. "He's in Oklahoma. For now." She shoved the phone in Lillian's face. "Here he is."

The guy was good-looking, Lillian would give Fran that. She nodded, hoping the proud mother would let it go.

"Did you want to get a hot cocoa?" Brody slipped his hand around her waist, lightly steering her in the direction of the beverage stand.

"Yes, please." She turned back to Fran. "It was nice meeting you."

Fran waved, narrowing her eyes at Brody's hand at the small of her back. "You, too, honey."

"You can thank me later." He spoke near Lillian's ear, sending a delicious shiver down the back of her neck.

"For what?"

"For getting you out of an awkward situation." He withdrew his hand as they joined the end of the line. "Imagine agreeing to a blind date with her son."

"People go on blind dates all the time." Why was she defending Fran? She had no intention of dating anyone. And blind dates? The worst.

"I saw the photo. The guy's got to be in his thirties. Something's wrong with him if he's still single at that point."

"You're over thirty, correct?" Lillian couldn't help pointing out his hypocrisy. Jonah began squirming. His pacifier was clipped to his sweatshirt, and she eased it into his mouth. He settled down quickly.

"That's different." His chin rose. He turned his attention to the large handwritten sign full of drink options.

"Why is it different?"

"Because I'm single by choice." Brody squinted at the sign.

"The lovely ladies you and your cousin were chatting up might need to be informed of that." Lil tightened her hold on the baby as he grew heavy in her arms. His mouth worked the pacifier as his eyelids closed.

"Who? Marissa and Jen? They're here visiting family."

"And if they weren't?"

He shot her a confused glance. "They'd be home. In Colorado."

She clearly wasn't getting through to him and decided to drop it. Brody ordered a black coffee for himself and a hot cocoa for her. The warm weight of the sleeping baby in her arms relaxed her.

"I'll carry this back to the booth." Brody hitched his chin to the baby. "Your hands are full."

"Do you know a lot of people around here?" She'd kind of assumed he knew everyone, but no one was stopping him to say hello.

"Not really." He lifted one of the cups over his head as three middle-school boys ran past. "I know some people by sight, and I'm starting to be on a first-name basis with others. That's one of the reasons I came today."

She wanted to ask the other reasons, but she didn't. It wasn't as if she was one of them.

"Look." She nodded to a table. "Local honey. And all those jams. I'm amazed by people who can make their own jams and preserves."

Lillian went over to check out the various flavors and eyed the pretty hand towels and quilted products. She addressed the older woman and teenager behind the table. "These linens are beautiful. You made them all yourselves?"

"Posey and I've been working on them since summer. She's coming along with her sewing if I do say so myself."

"M-o-o-o-m." The teen blushed and lifted her gaze to the ceiling.

"I agree." Lil couldn't stop admiring the ruffled edge of a Christmas tree skirt. "You're talented."

"Have I seen you around before?" The woman watched her more closely.

"Maybe. I've been attending Fairwood Community Church for the past couple of weeks. I'm Lillian Splendor."

"Grace and Posey Frye. We own a horse ranch west of town. Dale couldn't make it today."

"Dad didn't want to come, Ma." Posey turned to Lillian. "He doesn't like crowds."

"And who's your friend?" Grace asked her.

"Oh, sorry." Lillian turned to Brody. "This is Brody Hudson."

"You're one of Roy's grandkids. I heard you were taking over the ranch."

"Yes, ma'am." He nodded. "I'd shake your hand but mine are full." He raised the cups in apology.

"We won't keep you." Grace shooed them. "If you ever need anything, give us a call."

"Same here," Brody said. They kept moving until they reached Meena's booth, where there was a short line. Lillian carried Jonah between the tables and carefully settled him in the stroller, covering him with a light blanket. He wiggled twice and resumed his nap.

"Why don't we circle around the rest of the booths?" Brody handed her the hot chocolate.

"I should stay here and help Meena." She wanted to walk around with him, though.

"She's fine." He shook his head as if the concept was ridiculous. "Meena, you got this, right?"

Meena glanced up, grinning. "Of course!"

"See?"

"But the baby..."

"We'll take him with us. I'll push the stroller."

Lillian was out of excuses. "Lead the way."

He wheeled the stroller to the first aisle. As they made their way around booths full of homemade candles, wreaths, Christmas decorations and baked goods, Lillian made a point to compliment the vendors. She'd always been in awe of people who created the things she had no clue how to make.

With each stop, she learned more names and introduced

Brody, too. It was the least she could do for all his help. She wanted his transition to Fairwood to be smooth.

"I'm burning up in here." Brody ran a finger along the inside of his collar. "Can we go outside a minute?"

"Sure." Lillian was hot, too.

They made their way through the crowd to the entrance. As soon as they were outside, the cold breeze hit them, and for once, she didn't mind the drop in temperature.

"Look at the Christmas tree." Brody pointed to a tall decorated Christmas tree in the park. The gazebo strung with lights provided the backdrop for it.

"I didn't even notice the tree when we drove in." She rubbed her forearms. "It's beautiful."

"Want to go over there?" His wistful expression amused her. Reminded her of a hopeful little boy.

"Sure. Let me grab my jacket." She crouched next to the stroller and pulled it from the basket below. "Okay. Let's go. Oh, wait, Jonah's waking up. Hey, buddy." The baby reached his arms out for her, and she chuckled. "You're ready for a snuggle, aren't you?"

She unstrapped him and quickly put on his fleece one-piece. They checked for traffic and crossed the road. When they stopped in front of the tree, she and Brody craned their necks to see the top of it.

"It's bigger up close." He glanced at her and grinned. "Let me take him." He held the baby with one arm and pointed to the tree. "See, Jonah? There's a big star up there. And all those bulbs must have taken a long time to put up. Next Christmas you're going to be opening presents and eating cookies. We'll bring you back here. You've got a lot to look forward to."

That he did. They both did. Lillian discreetly took a picture of Brody holding Jonah and smiled at the photo. No one would guess that the man wasn't holding his own son.

Too bad Jonah didn't have a daddy.

"We'd better get him out of the cold." As Brody carried him back to the community center, Lillian debated what she wanted to do when the market closed at four. Since Sonny had all day Saturday and Sunday morning off from cooking, she could either make herself a sandwich and heat up a can of soup in her cabin or she could splurge on something small from one of the local joints.

"Have you been to Taco Tony's yet?" Brody held the door open for her, and she pushed the stroller inside.

"No. Where's that?"

"On Maple. It's tucked away. Easy to miss."

Sounded like a good description of her. Well, maybe that wasn't true. She'd been making more of an effort with people here. In Omaha, she'd go to work and run a few errands, but the rest of her free time had been spent at the apartment. With the communal dining at the lodge, she didn't have an excuse to stay in her cabin with Jonah all the time. Plus, everyone at church made a point to talk to her after services.

"Come out to dinner with me tonight." He paused and grinned. "My treat."

"I'll pay for my own meal." Why didn't she tell him no? She shouldn't be going out with him, but she didn't want to be by herself tonight.

The uncertainty in his eyes made her pause. "I want to pay."

"Why?" she asked.

He rubbed the back of his neck as people detoured around them. "Will you just let me?"

He was acting weird. If he wanted to pay so badly, she'd let him. It wasn't like this dinner was a date. And tacos did sound delicious. "Okay. Taco Tony's it is."

* * *

This wasn't a date, but it felt like a date, and he kind of wanted it to be a date.

Brody sat across from Lillian in the wooden booth that evening. Jonah's car seat fit on the bench next to her, and the baby was almost asleep again as he finished his bottle. Lillian had changed him while Brody and Hayden helped load Meena's supplies in the bed of Hayden's truck. His sister and cousin had ordered a pizza and headed back to the ranch. Brody hated admitting he was glad. He wanted Lillian all to himself.

And that in itself was strange.

As he and Lil had worked their way around the market, he'd been impressed at how she'd made a point to get to know the vendors, going out of her way to compliment them on their products. And she'd introduced him to them at every booth. Her genuineness drew people in. Including him.

"What are you getting?" She scanned the laminate menu. "I didn't think I'd be this hungry, but I'm starving."

"The Christmas market was a lot of work."

"For Meena." She met his gaze above the menu, and her blue eyes made his heart beat faster. "I don't know where she gets her energy. She almost sold out of the ornament kits."

"I don't know where she gets it, either." He decided on the enchilada platter and set the menu aside. "I take that back. Our mother. She's go, go, go."

Lillian placed her menu on top of his, then rested her elbows on the table, settling her chin on her clasped hands. "Tell me about your parents."

"What do you want to know?"

A waiter stopped by, and they placed their orders. The basket of tortilla chips and salsa were a welcome sight. He immediately dunked a chip and popped it in his mouth. So good.

"I don't know." She dipped an edge of a chip in the salsa. "Whatever you want to tell me."

He wasn't sure what to tell her. He loved his parents, but they'd always been more into their careers than their kids.

"Start with their names." She smiled at the waiter as he set two sodas on the table.

"My dad's name is Bill. My mom's name is Penny. They met in college. They're both parasitologists—biology researchers. They fell in love studying worms in petri dishes. That's how the story goes. Romantic, right? They got married during grad school, and we moved around a lot as kids."

"Did they both work when you were young?" She took a sip of soda.

"Yeah. We had nannies during the school year, and we spent our summers here at the ranch."

"Your parents didn't join you?"

"No. They typically scheduled their research trips for summers. As we got older, they accepted long-term assignments. That's why we rarely see them for holidays. Always on the edge of a breakthrough."

"They sound impressive."

"They are. They're good people. But they're difficult, too. Mom used to go in spurts trying to micromanage us, and Dad's always had high expectations for our careers."

"What was your degree in again?" Lillian asked.

"Agriculture science."

"They must be proud. Another science grad."

"Proud?" He let out a fake laugh. "No. I wouldn't describe it as proud. They wanted one of us kids to become a doctor, and I was their main target."

"Why was that?"

"I had the best grades. Plus, I was the oldest."

"Still, I'm sure they're glad you've turned out so well."

He didn't talk about this with people. Didn't think about it much, either. His parents were who they were.

Lillian made him want to open up, though. Maybe because she made him feel safe. He couldn't imagine her blabbing his secrets or looking down on him for his feelings.

"They don't like my choices." He kept his attention on the chip basket. "They were glad the six of us took over the ranch, but they weren't happy I quit my job."

"Why not?"

"They told me I was 'better than this.' They think I'm throwing away my career to be a glorified farmer."

She frowned and shook her head. "What? They said that?"

He replayed the phone conversation in his mind and didn't see why he couldn't spill it all.

"Mom told me to be smart. To hire a ranch manager and keep my job for the health benefits and retirement plan."

Their food arrived, and after thanking the waiter, Lillian leaned forward slightly. "What did your dad say?"

"That they didn't raise me to waste my life chasing around cows." He almost laughed at how absurd the conversation had been, but he and his dad had always been straight with each other. "I told him to say that to me the next time they went to a restaurant and ordered steak."

"You didn't." Her eyes danced.

"I did. He must have realized he'd sounded like a grump, because he mumbled that I was old enough to know what I'm doing. Both my parents wished me well with the venture before our call ended."

"Do they feel the same about Cooper and Meena?"

He took a bite of enchilada and chewed before answering. "Yes and no. Cooper has always done his own thing. He'll listen to their lectures, but nothing they say ever moves the needle if you know what I mean."

Lillian chuckled. "I do. He must be on the stubborn side. He seems quiet."

"He's reserved. Private. Brilliant, too. He knows all about the nutrition cattle need. I can't wait for him to move here."

"And Meena? Your parents didn't expect her to become a doctor, did they?"

"No, thankfully. My sister has always been a force of nature. Creative beyond belief. I remember her adding sequins to my basketball duffel bag one year. I flipped out. She never understood why I got mad. She claimed she'd 'matched the colors and everything.' My parents gave up on trying to box her in long ago."

"Good. She's amazing. I am in awe of her creativity and her energy."

"Aren't we all?" He loved his sister. "All teasing aside, though, she doesn't always get the approval she deserves from my folks. Mom hounds her to open her own business or move to a big city to make a name for herself."

Lillian tilted her head slightly, a thoughtful expression on her face. "I wonder why."

"For my parents? I think it's normal." He lifted one shoulder and dug into the rice. "They're overachievers and expect us to be, too."

"And you all are."

"How so?" He wasn't seeing it.

"You're all successful in what you do. And you're young. I can only imagine what you'll achieve on the ranch."

Her faith in them touched him. "You won't have to imagine it. You'll be here, too."

The tight smile didn't chase away the shadow that crossed her face. An uncomfortable sensation settled in his chest. Lillian wasn't thinking about moving away, was she?

She'd been researching apartments in town. That had to mean something.

If she pulled a Rebecca and left without saying goodbye and no way to contact her...

The hint of heartburn he was experiencing had nothing to do with the spicy food and everything to do with the fact he was growing too close to her and the baby.

He'd better start reminding himself why he was single. Why he had no plans to marry. Why he wouldn't chance another broken heart.

He couldn't trust Lillian to stay, and he couldn't offer her a good reason not to leave.

Brody hadn't even gotten up the nerve to find out why Rebecca had left him. And until he did, he doubted he'd get closure.

Maybe he didn't want closure.

Maybe he couldn't handle the truth.

"I'm going to find my own place, Brody."

"Here in town, right?"

She nodded.

"I wish you'd reconsider, but from everything you've told me, I guess I can understand."

"Accepting help doesn't come easily for me, and if it wasn't for Jonah..." She shrugged.

"You wouldn't have come here. I'm glad you did, though. When Rebecca left, I lost you, too. I'm glad we've reconnected."

But a part of him wanted more than her friendship. He was terrified of getting hurt, and he didn't know how to overcome it.

Chapter Nine

"I never knew Christmas cookies involved so many steps." Lillian sat on a stool at the kitchen island in the lodge as she watched Sonny roll out cookie dough. A bin held an assortment of metal cookie cutters, and she'd already examined each one. The reindeer was her favorite. Jonah was napping in his bouncy seat on the rug near the window, and Butch, wearing a festive bow on his collar, had sprawled out in a patch of sunlight next to him. "I always just bought a roll of sugar cookie dough from the supermarket—slice and bake."

It had been almost two weeks since the Christmas market, and she'd been hanging out with Brody after supper every night. In her living room, they'd decorated an artificial Christmas tree he'd found in the lodge's attic. A few days later, they'd decorated one in his cabin. They'd also been watching their favorite Christmas movies—she was partial to *Christmas with the Kranks*, while he preferred *A Christmas Story*.

Brody wasn't only a strong cowboy and natural leader. He was also dedicated to his family, the ranch and the cattle. Like Meena, he was creative.

Lillian was drawn to him. And she couldn't seem to halt her growing feelings for the man. From the way he went out of his way to sit close to her, she'd say he was drawn to her, too.

A few days ago, while Meena watched Jonah, Brody had

taken Lillian out on a UTV to see the herds. She'd enjoyed hearing about Herefords and Angus cows as he'd explained his theory about crossbreeding. His passion for cattle made her see the ranch through a different lens. He was a visionary and didn't seem to know it.

Last night after supper, he'd opened up about his struggles with Hayden over ranch decisions. They'd been clashing more and more. She'd started to tell him an idea but had shaken her head, claiming it was silly. He'd scooted closer to her on the couch, saying no idea of hers could ever be silly. His nearness had given her courage. She'd told him they should have to debate big decisions from the other person's point of view. To her surprise, Brody had actually been receptive to it.

"No premade dough here. No slicing." Sonny turned to her with a stern expression and a rolling pin in hand. "We make the dough and chill it before rolling it out. Then we sprinkle the flour, like so, to make sure the dough doesn't stick to the cutters." Sonny bent to check the thickness, gave one side another roll and stepped back. "You may begin."

Delighted, she moved the reindeer cutter to the edge of the dough. After pressing it, she lifted it, and the dough slid onto her hand.

"Good. Now set it here." He pointed to a cookie sheet. "When these two are filled up, we'll bake them."

They continued to cut out the dough, then Sonny slid the cookie sheets into the oven and started a timer. "We can't let these overbake. Light brown edges are what we're looking for."

She returned to her spot on the stool. The week after the Christmas market, Meena, Lillian and Sonny had decorated the lodge for Christmas in a burgundy-and-gold theme with a massive tree and evergreen boughs draped over the fireplace mantel. Lillian still couldn't believe the number of decorations it had taken. Every day, she'd been soaking in the Christmas cheer.

"How is the job search going?" Sonny asked.

"I got a call this morning from the hospital my friend works for. The one in Omaha. They want a second interview."

The sound of the door in the mudroom opening made her pause and turn. Moments later, Brody, his face ruddy from the cold, entered the kitchen and grinned.

"Christmas cookies? My favorite." He sniffed the air and closed his eyes. "When can I eat one?"

"They have to finish baking first." His presence filled her with joy lately.

"Lillian has good news to share." Sonny wiped his hands on a dish towel.

"Oh, yeah? What is it?" Brody stood to her left, not taking his gaze off the new batch of dough Sonny was rolling out.

She wasn't sure this was the right time to tell him, but when would be? And it wasn't as if anything was certain. "The hospital in Omaha called and requested a second interview."

The way his eyelids lowered, she wasn't sure he thought it was a good thing.

"Will you have to go to Omaha for the interview?" His voice sounded kind of strangled.

"No. It'll be a video call." Restless, she got off the stool and poked around the assortment of sprinkles in a container on the counter. She studied a bottle of pink sanding sugar, then set it down and turned to him.

"This is the work-from-home job, right?" He massaged the back of his neck.

"Yes."

"I'm happy for you." He didn't sound happy.

"Thanks."

"When is the interview?" Sonny asked as he bent to check on the cookies through the oven's window.

"Tomorrow."

"So soon?" Brody's voice rose at the end. "Would they hire you this close to Christmas?"

"I don't know." She hoped they would. The pay, in addition to Jonah's social security benefits, meant she could be independent sooner rather than later. She mentally ticked through the days. Only five left until Christmas Eve. "I hope so."

"You could ask them to wait to start after the new year." Was Brody put out about the job? She didn't know why he would be. What could he have against her working from home part-time to support herself and the baby? Did he want her to be dependent on him? She couldn't imagine him being so petty.

"If they offer me the position, I'll start whenever they want me to."

Brody stood. "I don't know, Lil. You've been through a lot. And you have the baby. The holidays are almost here. I don't want you overdoing it."

"I'm not sick or anything." Lillian glanced at Sonny, who was studiously inspecting the cookies through the oven door. "It's part-time. I'll manage."

Brody appeared ready to argue. He sighed. "Are you going to be free later this afternoon? I want to show you something."

"I have no plans."

"Great. I'll stop by your cabin in a few hours." He knocked his knuckles on the counter. "I've got to get back out there."

"Don't you want to wait for a cookie?" she asked.

"I'll have one later." He momentarily covered her hand with his. She was certain her face flamed to fire red. Then he left.

That was weird. She wiped flour from the counter as Sonny took both cookie sheets out of the oven.

"Perfection." He turned to her. "Now we wait until they've cooled before baking the next batch."

The side door opened again, and Lillian craned her neck to see if Brody had returned. Nope. Meena entered the kitchen. "Ooh, Christmas cookies. Are they ready to eat?"

"Not yet." Sonny gave her an indulgent smile. "Soon, though, Meena."

"I can't wait!" She rubbed her hands together and addressed Lil. "Oh, good. I was hoping I'd find you here. Can you get away for a few minutes?"

"I don't want to miss how to make icing." Lillian was enjoying her lessons in baking from Sonny.

"You have plenty of time," Sonny said. "I won't start the icing until you get back. Go."

She wanted to, but... "Jonah's sleeping."

"It will only take ten minutes," Meena said. "I promise."

"If he wakes, I'll take care of him." Sonny had held Jonah many times over the past two weeks, so she knew the baby would be in good hands.

"I guess I'll be back in a little bit then." Lillian checked on Jonah—still conked out—and thanked Sonny as she followed Meena to the mudroom where she'd hung her coat. Outside, flakes swirled, but they didn't seem to be sticking to the ground. She shoved her hands in her pockets, burrowed her neck deeper into her coat collar and hurried beside Meena toward the lane to the cabins.

"I finished Seth's cabin, and I wanted your opinion." Meena strode with her head high, taking in their surroundings. "Look! A cardinal. My favorite bird."

Lillian watched the male cardinal fly from a pine tree to a tall spruce. The flash of red amidst the snowflakes couldn't have been more Christmasy. Next week. And she wouldn't be alone for the holidays. She'd purchased small gifts for each of the cousins as well as a black apron for Sonny and a leather wallet for Brody. They'd all been so kind to her.

"With Seth's cabin finished, I'll be moving on to Cooper's." Meena's sure strides made quick work of the distance to the cabins. "I still don't get why Hayden won't let me touch his. It's not terrible inside, but everything's dated."

"Change must be hard for him."

"That's an understatement." Meena jogged up the porch steps of Seth's cabin and opened the door. Lillian wiped her shoes on the mat in the foyer.

"Wow. This turned out incredible." She couldn't stop staring. The walls had been painted a dark tan color, and natural hardwood floors completed the space. A small navy sectional faced the front window and a large television had been mounted to the wall. Three fluffy dog beds were lined up beneath the window. Behind the couch, large dog crates were tucked inside wooden dog houses, all painted navy and tan to match.

"You think so?" Meena studied the space. "Seth's a chill guy. Lives for the dogs he trains. I want him to feel comfortable here, especially since he's so used to traveling all the time."

"He'll feel right at home here." She joined Meena in the kitchenette, identical in layout to hers. "Does he own three dogs? Or are they ones he's training?"

"Seth owns one dog and typically needs space to take two others home with him. Not all the time. Mostly on weekends and holidays. When he moves, I'm not sure what he'll be doing."

"It's good you stayed on the safe side with housing the dogs." Lillian took in all the easy-to-overlook details Meena was so talented at including. Two stools had been tucked beneath the counter, and a charging station had been mounted to the wall. "I like this. He can work here if he wants."

"That's what I thought. He deals with a lot of spreadsheets and emails."

"Sounds like my old job. I spent a lot of time on the computer there, but with special software instead of spreadsheets." Lillian had always enjoyed that aspect of work.

"Yuck. Spreadsheets are boring."

They continued through the kitchen to the newly remodeled bathroom with white tiles and a wooden vanity, then peeked into the small laundry room and turned left into the large bedroom at the back of the house. The room was cozy and masculine with large windows and views of trees and distant snowcapped mountains.

"Did I miss anything? Do you think he'll be happy here?" Meena chewed on the fingertip of her index finger.

Lillian considered everything Meena had shown her. Then she mentally reviewed her impressions of Seth. He had an easygoing, patient personality. And his job training service dogs seemed to be what he lived for.

"What about storage for all the dog stuff? You know, toys, harnesses, leashes, treats, food?"

Meena's mouth dropped open, and her expression blanked. "You're right. I knew I was missing something." She smacked her forehead. "It's too late to install another cabinet."

Lillian returned to the living area and slowly circled around to study the foyer and kitchen.

"When Rebecca and I were tight on storage and didn't have much money, we bought an inexpensive cube unit. Bins hid all of our junk."

"Cube unit." Meena narrowed her eyes and tapped her chin. "Bins. Yes. I'm seeing it. That would work. Or I could order him a credenza." Her face cleared, and she gave Lillian a quick hug. "Thank you. You have the best ideas."

She frowned, ready to refute her. But Meena was already chattering away about how she was going to scroll through all her favorite home decorating apps until she found the perfect credenza.

"Hopefully, I can expedite shipping to have it here before Christmas." Meena was zipping her coat. "Can you believe it's next week already?"

"No, I can't. It hit me earlier that I've been here for almost two months. The time has flown by." Lillian put her gloves on. "Your brothers and cousins are all blessed to have you, you know."

"What do you mean?" Meena's nose wrinkled in confusion.

"You care about them. You pay attention to them. You're making sure everyone is comfortable here on the ranch."

"Well, of course." She smiled. "That's my job."

"No, it's not. You genuinely put their lifestyles first. You aren't simply decorating cabins—you're personalizing them."

They strolled outside and down the porch steps.

"I love my family." Meena gave her a sideways glance as they made their way back to the lodge. "I want us all to be happy here. And I want you to be happy here, too."

The words hit a squishy spot in her resolve. "I appreciate that, but as soon as I have a job, I'll be looking for an apartment in town."

"I wish you wouldn't."

For some reason, her serious tone pierced Lillian's patched-up heart. For most of her life, she'd felt like an afterthought. Another body to feed and clothe. Rebecca, of course, had changed that. And while Lillian had initially believed the

Hudsons were like any other foster family—helping her out in her time of need—she was starting to think otherwise.

Meena treated her like a valued friend, one she wanted in her life. And Brody... Brody had been treating her like one as well. And, if she wasn't mistaken, something more.

Lillian could no longer deny these people meant something to her. She'd grown close to Meena and Brody in a very short time. Hayden, too, to a lesser extent.

But was she reading too much into her relationship with Brody? She was falling for him. And even if he did share her feelings—which he didn't—it wouldn't take long for him to realize she was second best—a distant second—compared to Rebecca.

When was she going to wise up and remember how head over heels he'd been over her best friend?

Lillian needed to stop fooling herself where Brody was concerned. Nailing the interview tomorrow and getting the part-time job would be a good place to start.

Why wouldn't his cousin trust him on this? Brody stripped off his gloves and tossed them on the desk in the ranch office. Hayden had followed him inside, where he calmly took a seat in a wooden chair.

"I'm telling you we need the software. We invest now, and it will pay dividends for years to come. You're still trying to run this place like it's 1960. Things have changed." Brody dropped into the spinny-chair behind the desk and almost toppled over backward. He kept forgetting a spring had gone bad. Another thing to replace.

"New cattle, new software, new roofs on the outbuildings." Hayden gave him a deadpan stare. "You want everything new, but how are we going to pay for it all?"

Brody curled his fingers into his palms and directed his

gaze to the papers scattered around the desk. His cousin was too cautious, too tightfisted, and it was driving him bonkers.

"We've been over this—"

"Dipping into the rainy-day investments isn't wise. We need to preserve our resources."

Preserve our resources? Couldn't he hear himself? Even his vocabulary was outdated. His cousin needed to move into this century.

Brody opened his mouth to retort, but Lillian's advice trickled back. She'd mentioned debating each other from the other person's viewpoint. At the time, he'd wondered if it was realistic, but now?

"We've been around and around this multiple times." Brody lowered his voice. "Maybe we need to take a different approach."

If Hayden scowled any harder, his face would resemble a raisin. "What did you have in mind?"

Should he try Lillian's suggestion? He exhaled deeply. What was holding him back?

Not getting his way. That's what was holding him back.

He faced Hayden. "What if we tried an experiment?"

"What kind of experiment?"

"We hold a debate of sorts. You try to convince me, and I try to convince you."

"I thought that's what we're doing now."

"Ah, but there's a twist." He held up a finger. "I have to put myself in your shoes and convince you to do things your way."

Hayden grinned, leaning back. "I'm liking this."

"And you have to put yourself in my shoes and convince me to do things my way."

His smile slid away.

"Lillian suggested it, and I feel like we have nothing to lose at this point. I'm tired of clashing with you every day.

I want us to work out the big issues so we can focus on the day-to-day stuff. At this point, we're wasting time and energy without a long-term plan."

"What if this debate thing doesn't work?" Hayden angled his head.

Brody shrugged. "Then we try something else. Maybe we'll have the squad vote on it."

"Yeah, and if the vote comes out three to three?"

Brody ground his teeth together. Leave it to Hayden to find every potential problem.

"If it comes to that, we'll figure out a tiebreaker." Brody straightened the papers on the desk. He tended to let everything sprawl out. And Hayden liked things in tidy piles. If his cousin was going to trust him, he'd better make more of an effort to keep the office organized. Unless…

"Do you think we should each have our own offices?" Brody picked up a pen and tapped it against the desktop.

"Where did that come from? I thought we were discussing this debate thing."

"We are. I just… I know we have different organization styles."

Hayden stared at him with a confused expression.

Brody continued. "I mean, you like the door shut. No noise. And I like to hear what's happening. Plus, I don't mind papers spread out, and you're always filing them."

"Can we stay on task? It's hard to keep up with you sometimes," Hayden said. "I'm getting whiplash. One minute we're discussing one thing and then, bam! You bring up something else out of nowhere."

His cousin had a point. Brody gave him a sheepish grin. "My brain speeds ahead and goes off on tangents sometimes."

"I know, but mine runs in a straight line."

Were they doomed to always battle? Were their differences too big to overcome?

"What can I do to make it easier for us to work together?" Brody hadn't put much thought into the fact they had different thought processes in addition to their differences in opinions. "I want this to work out. You're my best friend. We've been given an incredible gift, and I don't want to blow it."

"You're right. We need to work this out, and we need to do it now." He sounded resigned. "I don't want to mess up this opportunity. I mean, I enjoyed being the ranch manager for Circle Seven Ranch, and I'll be the first to admit I got used to being on a tight budget with almost no room for error."

"You did a good job for them. And trust me, I respect the experience you bring to the table. We both know I don't have the patience for all the chores and day-to-day stuff you're doing around this place." Brody spent his mornings breaking ice and checking cattle in the pastures with Hayden or one of the other ranch hands, but after lunch, he handled the ranch's business and its investments. Hayden, on the other hand, repaired fences and treated sick cows and all the other physical work that came with a ranch.

Hayden sat up taller. "And I don't have the patience for all the paperwork and calls you handle. If I never have to make another phone call again, I'll be a happy man."

"We each have our own strengths." Brody chuckled.

"And our own weaknesses."

"True."

"I tell you what—if you want to hold a debate tomorrow the way you described, I'm willing to try." Hayden stood and held out his hand. "We good?"

"We're good." Brody shook it. They exchanged an understanding look, and then Hayden turned to leave.

"I'm checking on the steers. I'll catch up with you at supper."

"See you later, man."

After Hayden left, Brody checked the time. Perfect. He couldn't wait to show Lillian what he'd found yesterday. He closed the door and strode through the barn. Outside, snowflakes were falling, and he settled into a brisk pace as he observed everything around him, from the tall evergreen trees to the overcast sky.

For the first time since moving here, he had hope that he and Hayden would be able to settle into a solid working relationship. And he had Lillian to thank.

What if she got the job? A second interview meant they were interested. Why wouldn't they be? She was honest and dependable and...

Brody stumbled in a rut in the gravel.

She would get the job, and she'd be doing it from home.

But what if she got promoted? Would Lillian move back to Omaha and take Jonah with her?

He picked up his pace. These past couple of weeks had healed a part of him—the side that couldn't admit any weakness. He felt safe telling her things he'd never felt safe telling anyone, mainly because she didn't judge him. She offered her opinion, but that was different. He wanted her opinion, valued her input.

The cabins came into view. Every day the decorated porches got him into the Christmas spirit. He jogged up Lillian's porch steps and knocked on her cabin door.

When she opened it, his stomach dropped at the sight of her shiny black hair and those expressive blue eyes hinting at her inner warmth.

Lillian Splendor was beautiful. She took his breath away.

He'd have to deal with these sensations later. Pretend he

wasn't falling for her so hard that he was careening on a collision course ending in a brick wall.

What he was feeling for her was different from what he'd felt for Rebecca. He'd never felt this way before. And he wasn't sure what to make of it.

"Get your coat on." He hitched his chin to the hooks on the wall. "I'm taking you to the stables."

"The stables?"

"Yep." Standing in her entryway, he took in the open living area. "Where's Jonah?"

"Over there." The baby was in his bouncy seat grabbing for the toy bar.

"Want me to get him in his snowsuit?"

"Would you?" She shoved one arm in her winter coat, then the other.

"Bring him over—I don't want to track these dirty boots all over your floor."

Lillian untucked her hair from the coat collar, then went to the baby. She took him out of the seat and kissed both cheeks. Then she handed him to Brody and began putting on her worn snow boots. Little did she know with Meena's help he'd gotten her a pair of top-notch cowboy boots for Christmas.

"Hey, there, buckaroo. How about we get you in this nice, warm snowsuit?"

The child blinked at him. He took that as a yes. Brody dropped to one knee and laid out the snowsuit with one hand, then he positioned the baby on top of it and got him in it limb by limb. Jonah's kicking made it a challenge, but eventually Brody zipped it, rose and carried the child on his hip.

"Ready?" A stocking cap with a furry pompom covered Lillian's hair, and she wore knitted gloves.

"Ready."

"Do you want to bring the stroller?" she asked.

"Nah, I'll carry him."

As they ambled down the lane, Brody admitted that he and Hayden were trying her idea.

"You're really going to debate each other?" Her face seemed to glow, and he liked seeing her relaxed and happy.

"Yes. He has to convince me to invest in herd management software, and I have to convince him we can't afford it."

"Wow. I'm impressed you got him to agree. Who do you think will win?"

"Me, if I have any say." He glanced her way, and she grinned. "I'm going to get all the financial data for Hudson Ranch, Inc. tonight so I can present it in the most basic form."

"Smart plan."

When they reached the stables, they entered through the sliding wooden door.

"I'm curious what you want to show me. Did you get a new horse or something?" Lillian slowed as they passed empty stalls. Most of the horses were out in the pasture. A few sick calves and cows were on the other side of the stables. They'd remain there until they'd recovered enough to rejoin their herds.

"No. Not a horse." He carried Jonah to the last stall and turned to Lillian. "Okay. Here it is."

She scooted next to him and gasped. A spotted fawn was curled up in the straw. An evergreen wreath with a red bow hung on a nail above it.

"It's a baby deer!" Lillian's eyes sparkled as she glanced his way. "Where did you find it? Will it be okay?"

"I was out riding the other day. There's a gully a couple of naughty calves like to hide in, so I went over there thinking I'd find one of the Herefords. Well, I did not find that delinquent, but I found this little guy. And that in itself was odd. This is not the time of year for mule deer to be having babies. So I left him alone. Does are notorious for leaving their babies for long periods of time. Yesterday, I went to check on him, and I could tell he'd been abandoned. His backside wasn't getting cleaned by his mother. Not five minutes later, Hayden called me. He'd stumbled across a dead doe not far from there."

"Oh, that breaks my heart. He lost his mommy."

"This fawn has us now. We're bottle-feeding him, keeping him warm."

Lillian threw her arms around Brody's waist and held tightly. His chest swelled with pride as he kept a firm grip on the baby. "Thank you for saving him. Thank you for feeding him and giving him a safe bed in a warm barn."

Why did he have a feeling she wasn't only talking about the deer?

"Of course," he said huskily, awkwardly patting her with his free hand.

When she pulled away, her clear gaze captured his. He felt like he could see all the way through the years to when she was a child. And what he saw convinced him she trusted him—as much as she could trust anyone.

He didn't care that he was holding a baby. He didn't care they were standing in the aisle of the stables in broad daylight.

He bent his head and kissed her. Her sharp intake of breath made him move closer. He wanted to hold her. He wanted to protect her, let her soothe him. He wanted to run his hands down her arms and tell her that she belonged here. With him.

But he didn't. He ended the kiss, immediately wishing he could kiss her again.

"Why did you do that?" Lillian asked.

"Because..." He struggled to form an answer. "I wanted to. Are you mad?"

"No." Her troubled expression didn't convince him. "I'd

better take the baby." She reached for Jonah, and Brody didn't put up a fight. If he didn't get his head on straight soon, he'd be in a world of pain.

He knew exactly what the pain entailed. Because he'd been through it with her best friend.

Maybe he wasn't being fair to Lillian. She and Rebecca were different people.

He wasn't sure how to trust that she wouldn't break his heart. And he had unanswered questions about the past. Until he got the nerve to ask for answers, he'd best keep his hands to himself.

Chapter Ten

"Yes, I can start the first week of January." Lillian could barely contain her excitement the following morning as the interviewer went over her hours and the pay schedule.

"As soon as you sign the paperwork and take the drug test, I'll have IT mail you a laptop with the software we use."

"Thank you." They discussed benefits and chatted a few more minutes before ending the call.

Lillian stared at the blank screen of her phone for two beats, then let out a shout. She had a job! One she could do from home and that she could fit around her schedule. It paid more than she'd hoped, and she'd be using the skills she'd already learned from her years working at the urgent care.

This felt too good to be true!

She plopped down onto the couch and shook her head in wonder. Then she set the phone on the end table and bowed her head.

Thank You, Lord, for this job. Every time I worry and fret about how I'll get by, You provide for me beyond what I'd hoped.

So many things were running through her head she could barely keep up. Steady employment meant she could stay in Fairwood indefinitely. The relief pouring through her made her realize how worried she'd been about having to move away to get a job. She couldn't imagine starting over somewhere else at this point. Not with how close she'd gotten to Meena and Sonny...and Brody. Especially Brody.

He'd kissed her. An I'm-as-scared-of-love-as-you-are kiss. And he'd done it because he'd wanted to. It had felt right. With his strong arms around her and the baby, she'd felt protected and needed.

Besides Rebecca, she couldn't remember anyone ever *needing* her.

She stood and admired the Christmas tree. Part of her was glad the hospital didn't want her to start until January. It would allow her to enjoy the holidays and start seriously hunting for apartments to move into before spring. At the Christmas market, that Fran lady had mentioned her duplex becoming available soon. Lillian would give her a call—find out who owned it and what the rent would be. Although next door might be too close to the nosy woman intent on marrying off her son.

Lillian only had thoughts for one man. Ever since the kiss, she'd been waffling between dreaming of being Brody's girlfriend and facing reality. Even if he found her attractive or was drawn to her for the moment, she couldn't start pretending she was his type.

Back in college, he'd been drawn to outgoing, beautiful, charismatic Rebecca. And no matter what Lillian did, she'd never be any of those things.

She'd known since she was a young child that she was ordinary, and she was okay with that. She liked herself—she wasn't putting herself down—she was being realistic.

Rebecca had drawn people to her like a magnet. Lillian had always been easily overlooked, and she didn't mind. She was who she was. And who she was would never retain Brody's interest long-term.

Way to celebrate the good news, Lil, by making yourself feel bad.

She shook away the negative thoughts. Good things were happening—she had a job!

Should she text Brody? Let him know how the interview went? Her fingers hovered over the screen, but she simply slid the phone in her pocket. He'd been unenthusiastic about her job search, and for the life of her, she didn't know why.

Noises from Jonah's room alerted her he was waking up. She crossed through the kitchenette down the hallway to the baby's room and quickly restocked the diaper bag as he stirred. She'd promised Sonny she'd tell him how the interview went. Might as well go over to the lodge now. They planned on making more cookies all afternoon. She loved learning how to bake. And Sonny was so easy to talk to. Plus, it gave her a chance to love on Butch. She kind of missed having the big dog stay with her.

Lillian picked up the now whimpering baby. Cradling him to her shoulder, she soothed him and headed to the kitchenette for his bottle.

"It's not fun waking up, is it? You're probably hungry, huh?" She kissed his little head, enjoying the warmth of his cuddly body. "After you have your bottle, we're going to make cookies with Sonny again."

Twenty minutes later at the lodge, she settled Jonah into the baby carrier and greeted Sonny, who was sliding out the stand mixer on the counter. "Guess what?"

"You got the job?"

"I did." She couldn't help doing a little hop, and the baby pumped his legs in glee.

"Congratulations!" Sonny, being mindful of Jonah, gave her a high five, then patted the baby's head. "Tell me all about it."

Lillian relayed everything the interviewer told her as they began organizing the ingredients for the first batch of cookies.

"The position offers everything you need. Flexible hours, a steady paycheck, working from home." He pulled out a large spoon and handed it to her. "And to start after Christmas is great timing, too."

"That's what I thought."

They continued to chat as he showed her the recipes they were making and explained each step. Jonah reached for the bowl a few times, but Lil was too quick for him. "No, you don't. No yummy dough for you, mister. Maybe next year."

"I'm glad you've been baking with me, Lillian." Sonny sifted powdered sugar into a glass bowl. "I missed out on these times with Josie and her boys."

"What happened to cause the rift?" She leaned against the counter, noting the baby growing drowsy in the carrier. His energy came and went in bursts.

Sonny's glance was full of pain. "I spent Josie's childhood trying to make a name for myself in the restaurant world. Her mother left me, and I didn't prioritize visiting my daughter. We grew more estranged as she got older. I brought this on myself."

Sadness trickled down her core. It seemed like a waste for Josie to be estranged from such a kind, patient man like Sonny.

"If I had a father like you, I don't think anything could keep us apart."

He blinked, keeping his gaze on the growing mound of powdered sugar. "That's very kind of you to say."

"I mean it. I never had a dad." She measured oil into a measuring cup. "Do you know where Josie lives? Have you reached out to her lately?"

"I have her address and cell number. But I… I don't know."

"Why don't you reach out to her? Try to reconnect?"

"I don't want to cause her more pain." He set the empty sifter in the sink and sealed the bag of sugar. "What if she doesn't answer?"

"At least you'll know you tried." She tried to keep her voice from sounding judgy. Over the years, some of her foster siblings had been reunited with their parents. Initially, they'd be so excited—but they'd also clung to a lot of anger and resentment. Josie might not want to talk to him. "If you do reach out, she might have things to say that you won't like."

He let out a soft chuckle. "I'm sure she'll have plenty of things to say that I won't like. But I'd rather get yelled at and have her and my grandsons in my life than avoid a confrontation."

"That's a good attitude."

Christmas music played in the background as they baked thumbprints, chocolate chip cookies, peanut butter blossoms and spritz cookies. As the afternoon wore on, Lillian fed the baby again before settling him into his bouncy seat for a nap. Butch stretched out next to him.

A few minutes after four, male voices in the mudroom alerted her that Brody and Hayden had arrived. Meena was scolding them about something.

Adrenaline kicked in. Lillian might as well tell them about her job now while they were all here. As they entered the kitchen, Brody and Hayden were shoving each other's shoulders and laughing, reminding her of when she'd dodged boys in the high school halls. And Meena, chin up and shaking her head, marched in behind them.

Brody's attention was laser-focused on Lillian, and he strode straight to her at the end of the island. She tried to focus on applying sprinkles to the spritz cookies, but she couldn't think of anything beyond the fact he stood there.

Butch woke, stretched his furry legs out one by one and ambled over to Brody. The cowboy lavished the dog with pets, then straightened, staring intently at Lillian.

Her neck flushed with heat. She wasn't used to this level of notice. "Cookie?" she squeaked.

"Yes." He selected a peanut butter blossom and ate it in one bite.

"How did the interview go?" Meena rushed over to her, excitedly.

"Good." All the wonderful feelings rushed back. "Better than good. I got the job."

"That's great!" Meena enveloped her in a hug, rocked side to side and stepped back holding Lillian's upper arms. "I'm so happy for you."

"Thanks, Meena." Lillian shot Brody a glance. Deep in thought, judging from the lines in his forehead.

"Congratulations," Hayden said. "When do you start?"

"The first week in January." She explained how she could choose her own hours as long as the work was finished by a certain time each day.

"Seems we have good news all around." Hayden looked expectantly at Brody. "Why don't you tell them what we decided?"

"Oh, yeah, right." Brody didn't seem his usual outgoing self. "We've decided to invest in the herd management software. We're also holding off on some of the repairs to the outbuildings until next year. The roofs aren't in that bad a shape, and it will give us time to save the money and get competitive bids."

She couldn't help but smile. Brody and Hayden had been going round and round about the software and repairs since moving to the ranch. And they'd finally agreed on a solution.

"How in the world did you two compromise?" Meena took a bite of a cookie.

"We took Lillian's advice," Brody admitted. "Coming at the issue from Hayden's point of view helped me realize he was right about maintaining the rainy-day investments."

"And when I studied the herd management software for myself, it opened my eyes to how it could increase our profitability." Hayden exchanged an understanding stare with Brody.

"Good," Meena said decisively. "I'm tired of you two being at each other's throats. Maybe now you can work together more peacefully."

"We plan on it," Brody said.

No one spoke for a moment, and the oven timer dinged.

"This is the last of the cookies." Sonny set the sheet on the stovetop. "Now, I'm going to have to ask you to all leave. I need the space to prepare supper."

"Do you want an extra set of hands?" Lillian asked, brushing flour from her palms.

"No. I appreciate the offer, but I need to concentrate."

Meena and Hayden wandered out of the kitchen in the direction of the living room, and Lillian padded over to Jonah. She took him out of the bouncy seat while Brody grabbed the diaper bag.

"Can we talk?" he asked.

"Sure." She didn't like the phrase *can we talk*. Made her nervous. "Where?"

"Um." He wiped a hand over the back of his neck. "My place?"

"Just let me bundle him up."

Ten minutes later, they entered Brody's cabin. As cheerful as could be, Jonah blew raspberries. Lillian wished she had the baby's obliviousness at the moment.

"How is the fawn?" she asked.

"Good." He extended his arm for her to take a seat. "Warm, fed, sleeping. One of the barn cats decided to befriend him. They were curled up against each other when I last checked."

"Aww, that's sweet. What will happen to him as he gets older?"

"His spots are already fading, and that means he'll be able to survive on his own real soon. We'll probably release him in the woods near the path where the herd appears most often."

"What if he doesn't find the herd? He's so little. I hate to think he'll be fending for himself. I hear the coyotes at night."

"Hayden and I won't let that happen. We'll check on him. Don't worry."

Lillian perched on one end of the couch, holding the baby on her lap, and Brody crossed over to stare out the front of the window. Then he faced her.

"Lillian, I've been putting this off, but I can't any longer."

Her limbs stiffened as she braced herself for the worst. Her pulse was about to throb out of her neck, and for some reason, Rebecca's dead body flashed through her mind. How bad would this conversation be?

Serious announcements tended to bode ill for her.

She wished she could run out of there. Avoid whatever he was about to say. It would only hurt her. But she kept her gaze trained on him, hoping beyond hope she'd survive whatever he was about to say. From a young age, every time her life started to make sense, the rug was pulled out from under her. She had no reason to believe this conversation would be any different.

"I don't know why you getting a job is hitting me so hard." Brody had to handle this conversation correctly. He didn't want to create any emotional distance between him and Lillian, but he also couldn't take living with this uncertainty any longer. "Ever since you mentioned the second interview, it's been bothering me."

"Do you want me to be dependent on you or something?" She sounded curious, not upset. But, then, when did she ever sound upset?

Her calm demeanor, her way of adjusting to life as it threw wrenches at her, was part of what he found so attractive.

He wasn't sure if Lillian had learned to suppress the big feelings or was more adept at dealing with them than he was. He'd never been great at either.

"No. I don't want you to be dependent on me or on anyone for that matter." But was it true? Maybe he *did* want her dependent on him. Then he'd have some control. Not over her, but in being able to see her and spend time with her.

"I plan on working a few hours early each morning and again when Jonah naps. I won't need a sitter. The flexible schedule is more than I could have hoped for. I thought you'd be happy for me."

"I *am* happy for you." Was he, though? He cracked his knuckles, not sure why this conversation was so hard. "I guess I'm worried you'll leave."

Her expression blanked, then her eyes filled with understanding. He had to look away.

"Why does me leaving worry you?" The words were quiet, cautious.

"I haven't asked you some important questions." The way her eyelashes fluttered, he guessed she hadn't expected him to say that. Maybe his words were coming out wrong.

"I see," she said quietly. "I did promise. You're worried I'll leave without giving you answers. What do you want to know?"

He didn't know what he wanted to know. Did she have

feelings for him the way he did for her? Could they have a future together? Was she planning on leaving without saying goodbye? Would she cut him out of her life now that hers was back on track?

Did he mean anything at all to her?

Because she meant a whole lot to him.

"I suppose you want to know why Rebecca cut you out of her life."

Rebecca. Maybe he wanted answers to that, too.

His knees felt weak. He took a seat on the recliner and leaned forward with his hands gripping the ends of the armrests. He couldn't seem to form the right words. Lillian bounced the baby, who was drooling on his fist.

"Rebecca was never happier than when we were at Kansas State. From the minute she met you, she just floated, you know?" Lillian had a faraway look in her eyes. "As soon as she introduced me to you, I got it. You were perfect for her. And she was perfect for you."

He frowned, blinking. A few months ago, he would have eaten up those words. But now? He didn't know how to feel. Rebecca seemed far away. That entire chapter of his life had been fading more and more.

"Rebecca tried to keep up with her classes."

What? Where had that come from?

"What do you mean? She was getting straight A's." As the words left his mouth, he wanted to take them back. Why couldn't he get it through his thick skull that Rebecca had lied to him about a lot of things? She'd probably lied to him about that, too. And these revelations were no longer upsetting him the way they had when Lillian first arrived.

"She could have gotten straight A's." She widened her eyes. "Rebecca was smart, Brody. So smart. But she had trouble concentrating and didn't do well on tests."

"I never saw her study." Brody thought back to his time with her. They'd spent almost every evening together hanging out, watching television, going to college events. He'd assumed she was like him and managed to get her work done early in the morning and between classes.

"She couldn't keep her grades up, Brody. That's why she left. She failed out of college."

"Why didn't she tell me about her grades?" He wanted to stand, to pace, but why bother? All of this was in the past, practically a lifetime ago.

"I don't know. She probably felt like a failure. She'd been rejected by every foster family, including the one she'd done everything possible to stay with when she graduated from high school. College was her ticket to a better life, and when that was no longer an option—she became irrational. It was another loss in a life full of them."

The more details he learned about his ex-girlfriend, the more pity he felt for her. She'd been eighteen. Her upbringing had been unstable, and she'd been doing the best she could to make a future for herself. Who was he to judge her decisions? "I wouldn't have rejected her, Lil."

"I know you wouldn't. But she…" Lillian looked sick to her stomach. "I couldn't reason with her when she made up her mind about something."

"I'd have understood. She knew that, right? We could have worked something out."

"I know." Her eyes radiated compassion and honesty. "I told her that."

"I guess it comes down to a lack of trust on her part. She didn't trust me." He turned his face aside as he let his legs sprawl. "Why didn't you say anything to me? I could have used a warning."

"What was I supposed to say?" She sat up straighter, keeping a firm grip on Jonah. "They weren't my secrets."

"You should have given me a heads-up. You were my friend, too." His gaze locked on hers, and the curtain that dropped over her eyes made him wish he hadn't spoken.

"Would you go behind Hayden's back like that?" Lillian responded.

His spark of indignation snuffed out. He didn't bother answering. They both knew he wouldn't betray his best friend.

"By the time I found out, she'd made up her mind. It took me a while to learn how bad things had gotten."

"Define a while."

She focused on the crown of Jonah's head before meeting his gaze. "Exam week. I tried to convince her to tell you then. But she was in a frenzy. I could never get through to her when she was like that."

"What are you saying?" He didn't like the words she was tossing out, but they had a ring of truth to them.

"The Adderall, Brody. She'd take too much and wouldn't sleep. She'd be convinced she'd ace an exam, but she wouldn't actually study for it. She'd get the shakes. Her behavior scared me."

For the first time during this terrible conversation, he put his own thoughts aside and noted how it was affecting Lillian. She'd grown pale and had a troubled expression.

All this talk about Rebecca couldn't be good for her. He kept forgetting Lillian had found her dead body not long ago. That alone had been traumatizing enough. He shouldn't be causing her more pain.

"I tried to help her study. I begged her to contact her professors—I did everything I could. How do you think she got into college to begin with? *I* filled out the forms. *I* applied for our loans." Her voice was getting squeaky. "And *I* wasn't the one failing at the end of freshman year, Brody. Trust me—I had a lot riding on her getting good grades, too, and I tried to help her. I really tried. But no matter what I did, I couldn't stop her from finding someone who'd supply her with stimulants, and I couldn't make her sit down and do her homework. No one could."

She couldn't have shocked him more than if she'd slapped him in the face.

And he needed a slap.

"You dropped out of college for her, didn't you?" he asked softly. Missing pieces locked into place.

Her eyes held tears as she nodded.

"You took care of her through it all." So many things were starting to make sense. The things Lillian had told him since arriving at the ranch merged together to give him a more complete picture of her relationship with Rebecca.

"Rebecca didn't feel worthy of you, Brody." Lillian rose, shifting the baby to her hip. "She cut you out of her life because it was less painful that way. She couldn't handle you knowing the truth about her—from her life in foster care to her struggle with grades. And I'm sorry. Maybe I should have reached out and told you, but Rebecca was all I had. And it was my job to make sure she and I survived."

Lillian's cell phone rang. She immediately answered it. Brody tried to sort through the new information, and a profound sadness overcame him. Of all the scenarios he'd considered for ten years, the truth of Rebecca's situation had never occurred to him.

"Yes, I understand... There's nothing you can do?" Lillian's face drained of color. "Please call me with any updates."

She dropped her arm to her side and stared at him as if in a trance. "I think we're done. I've answered all your questions. I'm going back to my cabin."

"Who was on the phone?" He lurched to his feet and crossed over to her, wanting to put his hands on her shoulders, but he was too torn-up to chance it.

"The prosecutor in Omaha. Benny signed a plea deal. He'll be in prison for ten years, eligible for parole sooner."

"Is that good?"

She startled, meeting his gaze. "I don't know. I won't have to testify against him. But ten years?" She gave her head a small shake. "I have to go. I have to leave." She held the baby with one hand and grabbed his snowsuit, her coat and the diaper bag. She didn't bother putting on any of them as she stumbled toward the door.

Before he had time to react, she'd opened it and was jogging down his porch steps and then running to her cabin.

He stood with a hand on the doorframe, wanting to take off after her, but his feet refused to move.

He needed time to think, time to take in everything she'd told him. It wasn't fair of him to continue hounding her about Rebecca. Because he was pretty sure he'd broken his own rule and fallen in love with the woman who'd sacrificed so much for her friend.

Brody closed the door, shifted his jaw and went over to the couch. He had to sort things out, and he planned on sitting with his thoughts until they were sorted.

He didn't want to go back to the man he'd been before Lillian had shown up on the ranch. But he wasn't sure what kind of man he was capable of being. If Lillian didn't trust him—if she didn't think he could handle her past—she'd leave him, too, and at the moment, it was too much to take. He had to find a way to manage these feelings before they broke him.

The happiness he was flirting with was on the cusp of vanishing. And he didn't know how to prevent it. Wasn't sure he could even try.

Chapter Eleven

Once again, something bad had swooped in and canceled out the good. Lillian sipped tea later that evening as she sat with her legs curled on the couch in her cabin. She'd skipped supper at the lodge. Couldn't face Brody and pretend everything was fine. It wasn't.

The wind howling outside grated on her nerves. How Jonah could sleep through the noise, she had no clue. She doubted she'd sleep at all, but not because of the wind. Her nerves were crackling from her conversation with Brody earlier. And from the news about Benny.

Funny they'd happened at the same time.

The more she thought about Benny's plea deal, the more relieved she was that she wouldn't have to drive to Omaha for the trial. She didn't want to face the man who'd destroyed her life. She wanted to put all this behind her.

But she also didn't know if ten years was justice for someone who'd sold her best friend the pill that had killed her. Benny had murdered Rebecca, whether he'd intended to or not. He'd stolen her best friend, stolen Lillian's bank account and stolen her peace.

Explaining to Brody why Rebecca had left him had kicked up all the guilt and questions she'd been asking herself for the past months, if not the past decade.

Had she done enough for Rebecca? Had Lillian made the right decisions when dealing with her best friend?

If she'd responded differently when they'd left college and moved to Omaha—if she'd called Brody and explained what was going on—would Rebecca still be alive?

Brody would have shown up and helped them. Unfortunately, Lillian had known Rebecca well enough to grasp that she'd have considered it the ultimate betrayal. Rebecca might have cut both Brody and Lillian out of her life. And Lillian had been so afraid to lose her friendship.

She took another sip of tea and gazed at the lit Christmas tree with its pretty decorations. What about later? Like two years ago when Rebecca "quit" her job at the country club? When all the signs of Adderall abuse had been there? Sure, Lillian had begged her to get help. She'd given her pamphlets and texted her phone numbers of counselors and support groups.

But Rebecca had fervently denied being on the stimulants, going so far as to laugh off Lillian's concerns. She'd slunk away without pushing back. Then Rebecca had found out she was pregnant. Things had gotten real. That's when Lillian had ruthlessly confronted her about her drug problem. Their fight had been terrible. Rebecca had screamed that she was "being too controlling" and "you're not my mom," and she'd never forget Rebecca's parting shot of "who gave you the right to judge me?" Sure, Rebecca had broken down sobbing the following day and promised she'd stop, but Lillian had reached her own breaking point.

That's when she'd begun to distance herself from feeling responsible for Rebecca. She'd devoured articles and gotten advice from groups like Nar-Anon. And she'd prayed, relying on God to guide her, begging for Him to intervene with her friend.

Had Lillian been perfect? No. Had she done the best she could in her situation? Maybe. But at the end of the day, she had to accept that one big thing had always held her back.

Fear.

She'd been terrified that Rebecca would leave and cut all ties with her with no warning the same as she had with Brody.

Hadn't her fear come true, though? All ties had been cut between her and Rebecca. If death wasn't being cut out of someone's life, Lillian didn't know what was.

She placed her cup on the end table and went to the kitchen counter where her phone was charging.

Lillian owed Brody one more thing—and if she didn't deal with it now, she might convince herself not to. She stared at the dark screen of her phone, warring with herself. Should she or shouldn't she?

Closing her eyes, she swiped it and texted him. Are you busy right now?

A few moments passed. No. Why?

Could you come over?

Be right there.

Lillian drew her cardigan tighter around her body and drifted to the entry, flicking on the porch light. She silently prayed for courage. In no time at all, Brody arrived, and wind and snow blew inside as she opened the door. Quickly closing it, she waited for him to slip off his boots and hang his coat on the hook.

"Thanks for coming." Had her fingers turned to ice? "Want to sit down?"

She extended her arm to the living room, and they both took a seat—Lillian on the couch, and Brody on the chair.

"What's going on?" He scooched forward, bending to let his elbows rest on his knees as they splayed wide.

Her throat felt swollen; her tongue thick. How to begin this conversation? Staring into his caring brown eyes, she could no longer deny the truth.

She was in love with Brody Hudson.

It had been inevitable, really. He'd taken care of her and the baby when anyone else would have turned them away. Not only that, he'd provided for her, been a friend to her, opened his home to her, listened to her.

Do it. Apologize. Get it over with and get out of his life so he can find someone right for him. You're not it. You know it. You've always known it. You shouldn't have let yourself pretend otherwise.

"I'm sorry, Brody." She cleared her throat, willing the raspiness away. "I should have told you about Rebecca's grades before we left college. I could have at least contacted you when we got to Nebraska. I didn't because I was afraid. I didn't want to lose her."

"Did you think I was taking her away from you or something?" His eyebrows dipped low into a V.

"No." She shook her head. "I just knew her temper. I'd seen her cut people out of her life, and if I betrayed her trust, I had no reason to think I wouldn't be next. Mind you, I wasn't aware of any of this. I don't know that I truly understood my motivation until this afternoon when we talked about it."

His jaw clenched, and he remained silent.

She licked her lips and wrung her hands. "Here's the thing. Rebecca loved you. She never stopped loving you. And you two were perfect for each other. I always felt like she'd made a mistake by leaving. I know she'd have been a million times happier if she'd been honest with you."

"Maybe. Maybe not." He leaned back in the chair. That wasn't what she expected him to say.

"She would have been." Why did her heart feel like it was cracking? "I'm so thankful for you. I owe you a debt I can never repay. When Jonah and I arrived, I had no options. And you could have turned us away—anyone else would have, I'm sure—but you took care of us. You're like the Good Samaritan in the Bible, Brody. And..."

She couldn't choke out the rest. Maybe it was better to keep these thoughts to herself. No good could come from giving them a voice.

"I'm not a Good Samaritan, Lil." He got up and took the few steps to the front window, gazing out at the snow coming down against the night sky. "I've always liked you. I didn't *want* to turn you away. And, yeah, you should have told me about Rebecca back in college, but I understand why you didn't. And from everything you've shared since coming to the ranch, I don't know that she and I would have made it. A relationship has to be built on trust and commitment. We didn't have either."

Lillian wanted to say that he could trust Rebecca, and in some ways it would be true. But others? She herself had trusted Rebecca at a deep level, but she hadn't been able to trust her when it came to their finances or her substance abuse.

"I watched you two fall in love. It was love at first sight. You'd have done anything for her. And she wanted you to be happy." She stared at her lap. "If she were still alive, I'd still do anything for her. That's one of the reasons why I feel so connected to you. More than connected. You and I were the only two people in the world to get close—really close—to her."

He whirled to face her. "Don't do this."

"Don't do what?" Her heartbeat pounded as dread came over her. A clean break. That's what they were doing here.

"Don't try to sell me on a dead woman." His growly tone sounded less angry than tortured.

"I'm not. But I need to be honest with you. I've kept the most important things to myself my entire life, Brody." She rose, working out the kinks in her neck as she tried to get the courage to be honest. "I didn't dare speak them out loud. I've kept myself safe."

"You're safe here."

"Physically, yes." She'd give him that.

"In every way, Lil. You're safe." The intensity of his expression almost stole her breath.

"I don't know how to put this. I saw the real thing between you and Rebecca. And what you feel for me isn't the same, and it probably shouldn't be, but maybe I want it to be. I've never really given my heart to anyone... I don't know that I can. And I don't know why I'm saying any of this." She shook her head quickly. "I've got to live somewhere else. In Fairwood. Not here on the ranch. I hope we can be friends."

Saying the words broke her heart, but she couldn't stay here and fall in love with a man who'd never love her the way he'd loved Rebecca. Maybe now they could both move on.

But the ache in her chest assured her that moving on would be easier said than done.

Friends? She wanted to be friends? He blinked three or four times as his mouth went slack. She didn't think she could give her heart away. After she'd already stolen his. Because he loved her.

He'd fallen in love with her.

No, it wasn't head over heels like with Rebecca. But it was just as real. More real, in fact.

And try as he might, he couldn't bring himself to say the words. Four little letters were tripping him up.

What a mess he'd made of things by convincing her to stay.

"You're leaving." He'd known she would all along. "Cutting me out of your life the same as Rebecca did."

"No! That's not fair—"

"What is fair, Lil?" He stepped toward her. "Is it fair that I've mourned an idea of a woman for ten years? Is it fair that you dropped out of college for her? That you're raising her baby? Is it fair that no matter what I do to convince you to stay here on the ranch, you refuse? I can feel you pulling away. Rejecting me. I'm tired of hearing about fair."

"I'm not rejecting you." Her big blue eyes pleaded with him to understand. "I'm getting on my own two feet. I'm trying not to be a burden on you and your family. I'm protecting—"

"You're protecting yourself. I get it." All the things she'd shared about her childhood and past slammed into him. Why had he overlooked it all? Why had he thought he'd be the guy she'd take a chance on? She'd been tossed from foster home to foster home. Had given up her college dreams for her best friend—who'd died, leaving her baby behind. He didn't blame her for protecting herself. "You're cutting me out just like Rebecca did."

"I'm not Rebecca," she said with a hiss. "That's what I'm trying to tell you. I'm not her. I'm not beautiful and fun and compelling. I've been perfectly fine being her friend, the one in the background. Then I came here, and you're so..." Her face screwed up, and he wasn't sure if she was about to cry or yell at him.

"So...what?" He forced himself to speak gently. "What am I?"

"Perfect, Brody." She looked lost. "Absolutely perfect. And

I'm fooling myself if I think you could ever be content with me. I'll only remind you of Rebecca and all you lost."

"You're not Rebecca, and I don't want you to be."

"I saw what love looked like when you two were together. I know that's not how you feel about me."

"I know how I feel about you, and you're right, it's nothing like how I felt about her. It's deeper. It's more mature. And you and Rebecca are two different people."

"You wouldn't be happy with me."

"Shouldn't I be the judge of that?" He wanted to reach out and tuck her hair behind her ear, kiss her temple, tell her he'd keep her safe if she'd only let him. Instead, he kept his hands balled up by his sides. "You're scared like she was. You just have a different way of dealing with it."

She squeezed her eyes shut, shaking her head as if not wanting to hear.

"You're going to burn me." He stilled, accepting the truth, no longer daring to hope she'd take a chance on him.

"I'm not capable of burning you, Brody." Her head tilted. "You don't feel for me what you felt for Rebecca, and I can't live my life being compared to her and coming up short."

"I wouldn't do that." She wasn't even willing to try to work things out with him? And what did she mean, she'd come up short? His feelings for Lillian were real. But he couldn't say the words. Why couldn't he say the words? Frustration mounted—at himself.

Lillian exhaled loudly.

"The past ten years have changed me." He let out a huff. Why circle around it anymore? From her closed-off posture, he didn't have a chance. "When do you leave? Are you going to block my number? Delete my texts?"

"See? You always bring it back to her." She wrapped the cardigan around herself so tightly, he was surprised she could breathe. "I'll start looking for a place in town as soon as I get my first paycheck."

"Sounds like I have no say in this." He ground his teeth together, wanting to convince her to stay, but not willing to grovel. She'd clearly made up her mind and wasn't budging. "You've decided you're better off without me."

"You'll see it yourself in a few months." Her chin rose, and her eyes flashed. He wanted to take her in his arms and kiss some sense into her. But it would only make things even worse.

"I'll let myself out." He made quick work of getting his boots and coat on, then he turned to her. "What you and I have is different than what I had with Rebecca, Lil. But a few things are the same. Every morning, you're the first thing that comes to mind. I wonder if you slept well or if the baby kept you up. I look forward to seeing you at the lodge for breakfast. When I finish my work around the ranch, I get excited to share supper with you and hang out in one of our cabins. You're the calm to my storm, and I don't want to lose you. But I don't seem to have much choice."

He slipped outside and strode through the snow and wind. He'd made a mistake by taking in Lillian and Jonah. He'd fallen in love with her, but she refused to see it.

Love wasn't his thing. He couldn't say the words, and maybe that was for the best. If he suppressed it hard enough, it would go away. Wouldn't be real anymore. He couldn't win with Lillian Splendor, and he'd be best off forgetting her.

Chapter Twelve

She'd been keeping her distance from Brody for the past two days, and at this rate, her heartache was getting worse, not better. Lillian was practically choking on her love for him. She finished snapping Jonah's sleeper, picked him up and pretended to gobble his little neck. He liked that. Darling boy.

Carrying him into the living room, she ignored the gray sky outside and turned on the television to check the morning news. She'd been avoiding eating at the lodge altogether, and she missed Sonny and Butch. Meena had stopped by the cabin twice, and yesterday, Sonny had brought over leftovers from supper. He hadn't asked questions, but he'd assured her he was there if she wanted to talk about whatever was wrong.

She'd gotten teary-eyed at that.

Lillian could barely eat. Her emotions had been ripped apart and left in shattered pieces.

She'd made a rookie mistake. She'd gotten close to Brody Hudson, and she knew better than to become emotionally dependent on someone who would never need her the way she needed him.

Three weeks. Four, tops. That's all it would take, and she'd be out of there. She'd called Fran Bolenski about the duplex. It turned out Fran owned it and was willing to rent it to her for a rock-bottom price and only required half a month's rent for a deposit. Lillian had toured it yesterday, and the two-bedroom unit was old but clean and would suit her and Jonah for the indefinite future.

At some point, the whole out-of-sight-out-of-mind theory would kick in, and she'd be able to move on with her life. Maybe even get excited about it again. Maybe.

A knock at the door made her pulse race. *You know it's not Brody.* But she rushed to the door anyhow.

"What's going on with you?" Meena brushed past her on her way inside, and Lillian kept Jonah on her hip as she closed the door.

"Hi, Meena."

Meena unwound her scarf at record speed and scowled at her. "Don't 'hi, Meena' me. Something's wrong, and I'm not leaving until I have answers."

Ugh. This was the worst. But a tiny part of her perked up that Meena cared.

Lillian led the way to the couch, and Meena made a production of settling into the corner of it.

"Well?" Meena opened her hands.

"Well, what?" She'd play it cool.

"Why haven't you been eating at the lodge with us? Did something happen? Are you upset about the drug dealer guy making the plea deal? Or did we offend you?"

Lillian groaned. She hadn't thought about how her avoiding the lodge would be interpreted, and she probably should have.

"No, this isn't about the plea deal or anything." She set Jonah on his playmat and handed him a rattle. His feet kicked in the air as he shoved the toy in his mouth. Then she returned to the couch, staying within reach if the baby needed her.

"Then what is it?" Meena frowned. "It's Brody, isn't it?"

This situation got stickier by the minute.

"I knew he should have backed off." She pressed the meat

of her palm into her temple. "I told him you were mourning your best friend, but would he listen? No. And don't get me wrong, I want my big brother to be happy. And I know you would make him happy. But if you don't feel the same, or he rushed it, it won't work."

"Wait." Lillian wasn't sure she'd heard her correctly. "What?"

"Like it's a big secret." She scoffed as if making a joke. "We all can see he's smitten with you."

"No. He's been very kind. And patient. He needed answers about Rebecca, and I gave them to him."

"He hasn't been spending all his evenings with you to get answers about a woman who left him ten years ago. Lil." Her deadpan stare made Lillian squirm. "Brody is kind. But patient? No. Not my brother."

"He *is* patient. And Rebecca broke his heart." The words sounded thin to her ears. Brody had wanted answers when she first arrived. But as they'd gotten to know each other, he'd backed off. She'd been the one to tell him about the past. "He was just being nice to me. That's the kind of guy he is."

"I know my brother. He's not the type to *just be nice*. He likes you. He must have come on too strong. Do you think you could ever grow deeper feelings for him?"

The laugh escaped before she could stop it. Did she think she could grow deeper feelings? Hers were already so deep it would take an excavator to remove them.

Could Meena be correct about Brody having feelings for her?

What had he said? *The past ten years have changed me.* Lillian didn't doubt it. But the other things he'd said about his feelings for her being deeper, more mature? She didn't know about that.

"I have deep feelings, Meena," she said, picking at her leggings. "But I have to be realistic."

The way Meena's nose scrunched would have made Lil chuckle, but there was too much pressure on her chest.

"Realistic about what?"

She didn't know how to explain. Didn't know how to make it make sense. "I saw Brody with Rebecca. That was true love."

The way Meena was blinking screamed her skepticism. "And *I* see Brody with you. *That's* true love."

Could she be right? Could Lillian have it all wrong? Fear gripped her insides and twisted.

I can't lose again. I can't do this. I already lost Rebecca. If I leave now, I'll survive. But if I try a relationship with Brody...

Meena got up and sat next to her, taking Lillian's hands in hers. "What are you scared of?"

The woman was reading her mind. She tried to swallow the lump in her throat. How could she explain?

"One of my earliest memories was sitting in the living room of a foster home. The mom was on the phone. I heard her say, 'Yeah, I can take two boys, but you'll have to find somewhere else for the girl.'" She had to pause a moment. The memory still stung. Then she stared into Meena's eyes. "She told the person on the phone she could use the extra money, and she'd have me ready to leave by suppertime."

Meena didn't say anything, just squeezed her hands, urging her to continue.

"By supper, all of my belongings were in a trash bag next to me on the porch." Lillian pulled her shoulders back. "I learned from a young age that no one wanted me. I'm not telling you this to make you feel sorry for me. But my upbringing didn't exactly allow room for me to believe I could have a guy like Brody."

"Oh, Lil, I'm so sorry." Meena put her arms around her and drew her into a firm hug. "I'm sorry you went through that as a child."

Lillian was, too, and as she thought about that little girl sitting on the porch stoop with only a trash bag to her name, a profound sadness came over her. And the tears she'd been suppressing her entire life began to tumble out.

One dropped to her cheek. Then another. And she didn't want to cry, but she couldn't stop them from falling. Meena continued to hold her, rubbing her back, murmuring comforting noises.

When she was reasonably sure she could speak, she pulled out of the embrace. "I don't know if I have it in me."

"Have what in you?" Concern oozed from Meena.

"The faith to believe someone can value me."

"Lillian Splendor, you're worth your weight in gold." Meena put her hands on Lillian's shoulders. "If you have any doubts, open your Bible. Instead of a cradle, Jesus had a manger. Instead of a suitcase, you had a trash bag. Humble beginnings don't define you. Look at your Christmas tree."

Lillian wiped under her eyes with a tissue and turned to stare at the tree. She wasn't sure what she was supposed to be looking at.

"See the angel ornament?" Meena pointed. Lillian nodded. "Angels sang to shepherds near Bethlehem on the night Jesus was born. 'Glory to God in the highest, and on earth peace, good will toward men.' God chose *shepherds* to hear the angels singing. Shepherds. Do you get what I'm saying?"

A light began to glow from deep within Lillian's heart. "Yeah, I do."

"What am I saying?" She narrowed one eye, and Lillian let out a hiccup-laugh.

"You're saying my childhood doesn't define me."

"Not only that, but God was with you—He loved you—even then."

Lillian sat with that thought for a while. "That's hard, Meena."

"I know." She eased back. "It's hard to think God would allow you to grow up without a mom and dad to love you. It's hard to believe our loving Father didn't intervene when you were being moved to another home."

"It is," she whispered. "It's hard. But I see all the ways God took care of me, too. Even as a child before I knew Him. Before I found out about Jesus and realized I needed a Savior. I can trust God to provide what I need and thank Him for what I have."

"I don't know that my faith would be as strong as yours if our situations were reversed." Meena was biting the corner of her lower lip.

"My faith isn't strong. Some days it's as weak as a newborn baby. But I've learned to turn away from despair and cling to hope. God is full of love and hope."

"He is." Meena stood and stretched her arms behind her. "Why don't we go over to the lodge and snack on Christmas cookies? The boys aren't around. They're checking cattle or fixing fence or whatever they do all day. And starting tomorrow, this ranch will be a blur of activity with Seth and Kylie and Coop here for Christmas Eve."

Lillian hesitated. She didn't want to run into Brody. She didn't know what to say to him, and this visit with Meena had shaken loose the beliefs inside her that had been zip-tied into place long ago.

"I'm going to stay here. I've got some thinking to do."

"If you love my brother—and I really hope you love him—please give him a chance. Because, Lillian, he would never put you on the porch with your belongings in a trash bag. He's a forever kind of guy, and he doesn't give his heart away to anyone. Think about it."

"I will, Meena."

"Good. I'm taking off." She went to the entry and put on her coat. "Oh, did I tell you the credenza I bought for Seth's cabin arrived? It's gorgeous. Matches everything in there. Thanks again for catching the dog storage issue."

"You would have realized it eventually."

Meena tilted her head to study her a moment. "I don't think you have any idea how much I appreciate having you here at the ranch. We all do."

"Thanks. I owe you all a debt I could never repay."

"You owe us nothing." She wound the scarf around her neck, flipping her hair over it. "We're blessed by your friendship."

"Don't make me cry again," Lillian said, teasing.

Meena wrapped her in another hug. "I'm always around if you want to talk. I know I'll never be Rebecca, but I am your friend. I hope to always be your friend. You have a gift for making me feel accepted. Understood."

"Thank you. You have a gift for making me feel special." Her heart was brimming with emotion. "I hope we're always friends, too. You're one of a kind."

"Tell that to my family. They'll all be arriving tomorrow."

"Oh, they know."

They shared a warm look. Then Meena let herself out.

Lillian padded back to the living room and picked up Jonah. Meena had forced her to face things she'd locked up and ignored.

She needed to open her Bible. God's truth had a way of

overriding the things she'd been telling herself since she was a small child, and if there was ever a need for a reckoning, it was now.

"I'm tired of one-syllable answers, Brody." Hayden stood outside the steer pen where Brody was scattering straw under the lean-to. Brody had spent the past two hours cleaning out the manure and fixing the round hay feeder in the middle of the corral near the barn. Gave him something to do. Took his mind off the fact his love for Lillian was spiraling out of control, and he didn't have the guts to do a thing about it.

"Huh?" He stabbed the pitchfork into the bale.

"See?" Hayden opened the gate and strode to him. "Put the pitchfork down. They have enough straw."

"I'm not done." He pointed to the half bale.

"Leave it. They'll just toss it around like rowdy teens, anyhow."

He glared at Hayden and marched past him to the gate. His cousin quickly followed.

"Did you and Lillian get into a fight or something?"

"No!" Brody grimaced. "Why?"

"I thought…" Hayden frowned. "You two are close, and I thought—"

"We're not close. Not like that." He shouldn't be lying to his best friend.

"Could have fooled me."

Brody strode out of the pen, tossed his filthy gloves on the ground and continued to the barn. Hayden stayed right beside him. He marched through the barn and yanked open the office door. Went behind the desk and spun to face Hayden. "I fell in love with her."

Hayden's face brightened. "Good."

"Bad."

"What's the problem?"

"I can't tell her." He couldn't take his gaze off his hands planted on the desk.

"Why not?"

"She's moving into an apartment in town soon."

"And?"

It took every bit of self-control he could muster not to shout at Hayden. "I told her to stay here."

"I get that dating won't be as convenient with her in town, but—"

"She'll leave." There. He said it.

"What are you talking about?"

"There's nothing keeping her here, Hayden. She's already putting distance between us. One day I'll be feeling great, and I'll drive to her apartment, and it will be empty. No warning."

"Lillian doesn't strike me as the type, Brody." Hayden took out a chair and sat in it.

"Well, Rebecca didn't strike me as the type, either."

"Oh." A knowing look crossed his face. "You're comparing her to your ex."

"Her best friend." His voice rose. "Also a product of the foster-care system."

"Wow. You're losing it."

"Am I, Hayden?" he said. "Am I?"

"Yes." He nodded repeatedly. "You're scared."

"Of course I'm scared. Why wouldn't I be scared?" He pinched the bridge of his nose, then swiped his eyebrows with his finger and thumb. "I don't think I can do this."

"Does she know how you feel about her?"

How could Hayden look so calm and relaxed sitting there? Brody sank into the chair behind the desk and stared at the corner of the ceiling.

"I don't know."

"You haven't told her you love her?"

"Correct."

"And you're sure you love her?"

He glared at Hayden, who brought his hands, palms out, near his chest.

"Okay, okay. We won't discuss the L word. You're obviously getting signals from her that are making you worry."

Was he getting signals from Lillian? "I wouldn't say that. She's been up front about her plans all along." She'd been telling him for weeks that she was looking for a job and planned on settling in Fairwood.

"Good to know." Hayden raised his thumb. "But she's similar to Rebecca, right? That's why you're certain she's going to take off without telling you?"

Brody rubbed his temple. He was getting a headache. "She's nothing like Rebecca."

The sounds of cattle mooing far away filled the room for a few moments.

"Let's approach this from a different angle." Hayden was really getting on his nerves. Couldn't he let it be? "What don't you trust about her?"

He opened his mouth, but nothing came to mind.

"Take your time."

Brody ticked through everything he knew about Lillian. Her childhood. Her friendship with Rebecca. The way she'd stuck to her side and made difficult choices to be there for her.

All Lillian seemed to do was sacrifice. She was the most trustworthy woman he'd ever met.

"I trust everything about her," Brody said quietly.

"There you go. Problem solved." Hayden stood, turning to the door. "I'm getting back to my chores. What are you waiting for? Go tell her."

It wasn't that easy. Brody breathed a sigh of relief when Hayden left.

Lillian had opened up to him when it had been hard for her. Sure, he figured she'd left a lot of things unsaid. He'd barely scratched the surface in telling her how he felt. But at least she'd had the courage to be honest with him.

He hadn't even been honest with himself.

When it came down to it, he'd used Rebecca leaving him as an excuse to not get close to any woman. Then Lillian had arrived. He'd thought he'd needed answers—and maybe he had needed them. Maybe he'd needed to learn the truth about who Rebecca was in order to move on. She'd been young—a teenager—when they'd met. Not many people had their lives together at that age. He shouldn't have judged her so harshly.

While he felt bad for what Rebecca had been through, he felt worse for what Lillian had gone through. She'd been handed a lousy start to life and dealt with hurdle after hurdle as an adult. He wanted to be the man who took some of the load off her shoulders.

But how could he be that man if he couldn't even admit to her that he loved her?

He had a lot of soul-searching to do. He couldn't stand the thought of making this situation worse. Lillian deserved better than that. And maybe he did, too.

Chapter Thirteen

Later that night, Lillian closed the Bible and set it on her nightstand. She snuggled under the covers and stared at the ceiling. *God, I'll probably never know why my childhood was so broken. I'm afraid my adulthood is destined to be broken, too. That's why I'm scared of these feelings for Brody.*

The Bible passages she'd been reading raced around her mind. She'd found reference after reference to God commanding people to take care of the fatherless and the widows. How God Himself would be a Father to the fatherless and defend their cause.

Lillian had read through Luke, chapter two, as well. How the angels appeared to the shepherds. Just like Meena had said.

Then she'd thought about all the things she'd say to Rebecca if she'd lived. And the only thing she could come up with was *I miss you, Bec. I loved you. I needed you. I wish you were still here.*

She'd worried that she'd want to rage at her for her poor choices or for putting Lillian in a tight spot so many times. But none of it mattered. None of it had really ever mattered to her.

Being Rebecca's best friend had been enough.

And that realization had brought her to another one.

Lillian had confided things to Brody she'd never told anyone else. She trusted him. She loved him. And she wasn't going to leave without telling him.

Even if he lost interest in her. Or changed his mind about her. She was going to try to work it out.

He did love her, didn't he?

Maybe he hadn't said the words, but his actions had proven it. Meena was right about that, too. He acted like a man in love.

In Lillian's world, actions spoke louder than words.

How could she convince him she wasn't going to leave him? That she'd never cut him out of her life? If they parted ways, they'd both be fully aware of the reasons why.

Maybe a good start would be to stay on the ranch. They could continue to get to know each other, and in time, he might be able to handle his feelings for her.

She didn't blame him for struggling. In some ways, it made her love him all the more. He didn't open up to women lightly. He took his romantic life seriously.

The one thing she worried about was herself. If she couldn't accept that Brody could love her like he'd loved Rebecca, she didn't think they had much of a chance.

And she wasn't sure she could get there. Rebecca had been such a bright light.

But she'd hidden the dark parts.

Didn't everyone?

Rebecca had lacked the courage to show Brody who she really was. Lillian had been open with him from day one, and he'd gotten closer and closer to her. That had to count for something, right?

Tossing the covers back, she got out of bed. *I have to let this inferiority complex die. I can't keep comparing myself to her and coming up short.*

She padded down the hall to the living room. Turned on the Christmas tree lights. Sat on the couch, drawing her knees to her chest.

If Rebecca were here, what would she have to say?

Lillian could picture her big smile. Could imagine exactly what she'd say. *Lillian, the only reason you aren't dating anyone is because you're not out there. You work, you come home. That's it. If guys knew you the way I know you? They'd be tripping over themselves trying to date you.*

There was some truth to that. Lillian had never made an effort to meet guys. She'd been quietly surviving.

Could she do more than survive? Could she have a fuller life with Brody and the Hudson family?

Her instincts told her it was hers for the taking. But she had to accept it. Had to embrace it.

Instead of imagining Rebecca, Lillian pictured Meena talking to her. Brody's sister would say something along the lines of *How can I convince you to stay? We're all lost in our own way, Lil. Brody needs you.*

Wait. The Hudsons weren't lost. Meena certainly wasn't.

Conversations with Brody trickled back. About his parents. Their dedication to their research. How they never visited the ranch. How they wouldn't be there for Christmas.

She stilled. She'd missed it—a clue into his personality. Into all their personalities.

In some ways, all six of them had grown up missing something. Sure, they'd had each other. But their parents—both sets from the sound of it—had largely left their care to nannies during the school year and their grandparents during the summer.

No wonder they'd all decided to move here. They'd been relying on each other from a young age.

Lillian finally got it. They weren't including her out of charity or pity.

At some level, they understood what it was like to not be a priority. To take second place behind their parents' careers and interests.

And they'd chosen differently.

They'd chosen each other.

And they'd chosen her.

Excitement and hope and joy swirled inside her chest, bringing her to her feet. *God, thank You for leading me to the truth. Thank You for showing me a different perspective.*

As she returned to her bed, the angels' song ran through her head, *"Glory to God in the highest, and on earth peace, good will toward men."*

Lillian wasn't second best. She wasn't easy to overlook. She wasn't any of the things she'd believed.

She was God's child. And she was going to start acting like it.

A few minutes after midnight, Brody directed the flashlight down the main aisle of the stables. For hours, he'd been thinking about his conversation with Hayden. He'd skipped supper, and Meena had pounded on his cabin door until he'd opened up. She'd pushed her way inside, typical Meena style, and told him he needed to get his act together where Lillian was concerned. Then she'd shoved a foil-wrapped plate into his hands and commanded him to eat before stalking outside in a huff.

He'd eaten the meatloaf and potatoes, but he couldn't say he'd enjoyed them. And they were typically a favorite of his. How could he taste anything with such an awful burden hanging over him?

The burden had a name, and its name was Coward.

Brody had always patted himself on the back for his take-charge personality. He'd regularly been the first person to volunteer for any tough task.

But telling Lillian he loved her? Asking her to be his girlfriend?

The idea was killing him, and he didn't even know why.

When he reached the end, he peeked in on the fawn. Curled up in the straw with two cats. That deer grew in popularity with the strays each day. Too bad the cats would have to find a friend elsewhere. The fawn's spots had faded. He and Hayden would be setting it free tomorrow to give it its best chance at a normal life.

He backtracked down the aisle. If he could shift his thoughts away from Lillian, maybe he'd feel better. Cooper would be here tomorrow morning. Kylie and Seth were arriving in the afternoon.

What were his parents doing for Christmas Eve? He snorted and slid open the door to exit the building. After locking it, he burrowed his chin into his collar. His parents would be examining every aspect of some parasite on a petri dish and completely oblivious to the fact it was Christmas.

When had those two ever taken a vacation? A real vacation where they relaxed and didn't talk constantly about their research?

He couldn't remember a time.

The cold seeped through him, and he didn't care. He hated this wishy-washy feeling. He hated the uncertainty. He wanted his take-charge personality back.

Brody made his way down the lane toward the cabins. Memories of waiting for his parents to come home from the lab every Christmas Eve rushed back. He'd learned from a young age anytime they went to the lab, they lost track of time. The three kids would be stuck with a surly babysitter who'd only taken the job for the promise of triple the pay.

It had been up to Brody to make the day special for his siblings, and he'd done his best. They'd played games, watched Christmas movies, even made forts out of blankets in the family room.

He stared up at the stars and couldn't help smiling. Those Christmas Eves had been fun. But his parents had missed it all. Why hadn't they ever been able to tear themselves away from their research? Sure, on Christmas Day, they'd make a production out of opening presents. But by the afternoon, they'd be discussing their research once more.

Brody kicked at the gravel, sending a spray in the air. They were still missing out. They could have flown in for a day or two. Uncle Tony and Aunt Joanne had no excuses either.

He slowed his pace and finally did what he'd been avoiding for hours. He prayed.

God, what am I supposed to do? Why can't I tell Lillian how I feel about her? Am I still hung up on Rebecca?

He gazed at the crescent moon. Found the Big Dipper. And waited.

Maybe he was being unrealistic.

I got used to my parents not being around. And being with Rebecca made me feel wanted. But she left me. I wasn't enough for her. Just like I wasn't enough for my mom and dad.

Brody wasn't sure if the pressure behind his eyes was from the cold or from his emotions. He'd never realized he'd felt unimportant to the most important people in his life, excluding the squad.

But Lillian...

Lillian was steady. She made sacrifices—huge sacrifices—for her loved ones. She'd been honest with him. She didn't hide her true self the way Rebecca had.

Lillian would never leave him and cut him out of her life. She didn't have it in her.

The truth spiraled around him. He'd been searching for someone like her his entire life, and now that she was here, he was afraid she'd let him down, too. Afraid they'd grow close and she'd see whatever his parents and Rebecca had seen in him that made them shove him aside.

But he'd been looking at it all wrong. His perception had been skewed.

His parents loved him in their own way. And Rebecca had loved him, too.

He'd assumed Rebecca left because she grew tired of him, but Lillian had shown him the truth, that she'd left due to her own insecurities.

God, I'm ready to let her go. I'm ready to let my disappointment about my parents go, too.

He had the real deal with Lillian. A loyal friend. A beautiful woman. A partner in life...if he could get the guts to give her the space she needed.

It was time to do the hard things. Time to trust God with his future. Starting this morning.

Chapter Fourteen

"Merry Christmas Eve."

Lillian's mouth curved into a smile at the sight of Sonny and Butch on her porch step the following morning. She kept a tight grip on the squirmy baby. "Merry Christmas Eve to you, too. What are you doing here?"

Butch wagged his tail and ambled inside, sniffing Jonah's tiny socks covering his feet. The baby started making babbling noises, clearly loving the dog's attention.

"Brought you a little something." He held up a cardboard box that bakeries typically used.

"You didn't have to do that." She stepped back and to the side. "Come in."

"I don't want to keep you."

"From what?" She chuckled. "Folding onesies? Get in here."

"Well, maybe for a minute." His merry eyes creased in the corners as he entered. After toeing off his boots, he continued straight ahead to the kitchen where Lillian pulled out two mugs.

"You'll stay for a cup of coffee, won't you?" she asked.

"Sure." He took out a stool and lowered his frame on it. "We missed you at breakfast. Again."

She took out cream and sugar, setting them on the counter, before pouring two mugs. She handed him one and stood with the counter between them. Sonny opened the box and gestured to the pecan rolls and cookies.

Lillian selected one of the rolls, but Jonah started to fuss, so she excused herself to get him settled in his bouncy seat. His fussing turned to happy gurgles as he kicked his feet and reached for the toy bar.

"I'm sorry I haven't been around." She tore a section off the roll and took a bite.

"Did something happen with the job?"

"No. The job is a go. And I found out Benny agreed to a plea deal. I don't feel like justice is being done, but it is a relief to not have to go back to Omaha and testify."

"I get that." He took a sip. "You're missing Rebecca, aren't you?"

"Yes." Shouldn't she be more open with him? She considered him a friend. "But that's not why I've been staying in the cabin. It's Brody. My relationship with him is complicated."

"Because he was in love with your friend."

"Yes. And for other reasons."

"You care for him. And he cares for you."

She winced. Why did hearing confirmation that Brody cared for her make her uncomfortable? "Yes."

"What's holding you back?"

Her prayers and revelations from yesterday were still fresh in her mind. "Hopefully, nothing will hold me back. I've been working through some stuff."

"Ahh. Good. Good for you. I've been working through some stuff, too."

"Really?" She focused on him and saw there was a hint of fear—and hope—in his eyes. "Like what?"

"You first." His face was etched with wisdom and patience.

Once more, Lillian wished she could have had a father like him growing up.

"When I arrived here almost two months ago, I was at the lowest point of my life. My best friend had died, my apartment had been robbed, my bank account wiped out, and I had a baby to raise. To say I felt unworthy of the Hudsons' kindness is understating it. And Brody, especially—we had issues."

"I know."

Of course he knew—she'd told him most of it. "But Brody and I have become good friends. And maybe more. I've been struggling to trust it."

"Why? He's a good one, Lil."

"That's why. He *is* a good one. The best one. And I'm... not."

"You're a good one, Lil. The best one."

"I haven't felt worthy."

"You are worthy."

"I know. In God's eyes, I am."

"In everyone's eyes. Everyone around here, at least." He adjusted the cuff of his sweater. "Are you going to tell him how you feel?"

"I'm trying to work up the nerve." Speaking of nerves, hers were going haywire at the thought of seeing Brody again.

"Christmas is the season of hope. With that in mind, I'm working up the nerve to reach out to Josie."

"You should." She brought her hands to the prayer position near her chest. "Absolutely."

"Then you should, too." He began to stand. "Love is a gift, Lillian. Accept it. Embrace it. Don't hide from it, or you'll end up like me. Old, alone and full of regrets."

"You're not alone, Sonny." Lillian rounded the counter, took his hand and squeezed it. "You have me."

He returned the squeeze. "And you have me."

They shared an understanding look.

"You're calling her today, huh?" Lillian followed him to the entry. He bent to put on his boots, glancing up at her.

"Yes. Right now. I'm going back to my house and calling her."

"Then I'd better figure out a plan, too."

"Text him to come over. Tell him how you feel."

Lillian curled her lips. "I'm not ready."

"We never are. Don't wait. You're more courageous than you give yourself credit for."

"Thanks, Sonny." She gave him a light hug and waved goodbye. Then she closed the door and let her back rest against it. How was she supposed to go about this?

She knew what she needed to say. She loved him and wanted to stay on the ranch. But she didn't want him to feel trapped. What if it didn't work out?

Maybe she needed to shower and put on a decent outfit. Do her hair and throw on some makeup.

If she was telling Brody she loved him, she wasn't doing it with baby spit-up on her shirt and wearing stretched-out sweatpants.

"You are coming with me, little man." She picked up Jonah and brought him and the bouncy seat into the bathroom. Then she showered, picked out a pretty sweater and dark jeans and proceeded to blow dry her hair.

By the time she'd applied makeup and fed Jonah his bottle, she was exhausted.

What if she told Brody how she felt, and he dismissed her feelings? Their last conversation had been heated. Whatever he might have felt for her could be gone. Or maybe he remembered Rebecca and realized he'd made a mistake spending so much time with Lillian.

She returned to the living room. With her phone in her hand, she debated what to do. Call him? Text him? Pretend she hadn't fallen in love with him so hard she could barely wrap her head around the fact he might love her, too?

Courage, Lil. She'd better talk to him before Cooper, Seth and Kylie arrived. And if the conversation didn't go well? She'd celebrate Christmas here in her cabin with Jonah. Alone.

"Meena, I need you to go to Lillian's cabin and babysit Jonah." Brody stood in Meena's cabin—not remodeled yet, and he had no idea why since she was the one refurbishing the cabins—and pointed in the direction of Lil's cabin. "Hayden, did you map out the best spot in the woods?"

Holding a box of chocolates near the couch, Hayden popped a candy in his mouth and nodded.

"Hey, don't eat all my Godivas." Meena reached for the box, but Hayden held it above his head. "Brody? Help me out here?"

Brody glared at Hayden. "Give them back. You know how she gets when you take one of her favorites."

"I didn't touch the mint medallion." Hayden lowered the box, and Meena snatched it from him. "Promise."

"You better not have," she mumbled, scrutinizing the remaining candies.

"People. Focus." Brody clapped his hands. "The chocolates aren't important. Lillian is."

Meena sighed. "You're right. I'll go over there. But what if she won't let me watch the baby?"

"I'll kidnap her if I have to." Brody craned his neck, keeping an eye on Lillian's front porch from the front window.

"No kidnapping. No police." Hayden thrust his hands out.

"Our first Christmas together owning the ranch should be memorable, but not *that* memorable."

"It was a figure of speech." Why were these two so intent on annoying him? He was stressed out enough as it was. "Did you find the path the mule deer take or not?"

"I did. Marked the best drop-off spot with yellow flag markers. You can't miss it."

"Good." He narrowed his eyes, rubbing his hands together. "When does Cooper arrive?"

Meena checked her phone. "In two hours."

"Kylie and Seth?"

"Around four-thirty," she said.

"Okay. Then we're all set. Any questions?" Brody looked at Hayden, then Meena.

"I have a lot of questions." Hayden's dry tone raised Brody's hackles. "But they can wait. I'll get the UTV ready with the big crate."

"Thanks, man."

"Are you going to wear that?" Meena turned up her nose.

Brody looked at his flannel shirt and jeans. "Yeah, why?"

She let out a disgusted breath and shook her head. "No. Go change into the sweater I bought you last year and your good jeans. Are you trying to impress her or not? And spray on some cologne."

He gave her a sheepish smile. "Okay. Thanks, Meena."

"I'm heading over there now." Meena went to the mat where boots and shoes were lined up. "Make yourself presentable."

"I'll be there in ten."

"Teasing aside—" she straightened "—I'm glad you're doing this. I love seeing you happy."

"We'll see how today goes." He rubbed the back of his neck as his cheeks grew warm.

"Patience. She's not used to being essential to anyone." She patted his cheek. "Go. Change."

He pulled her into a hug. "Thanks."

Essential. Yes, that described how he felt about Lillian. She'd become essential to him.

Outside, he shoved his hands in his coat pockets and strode to his cabin. He made quick work of making himself presentable and headed over to Lillian's.

He'd spent ten years refusing to consider love. And the past three days had convinced him he couldn't live without it. Now he had to make Lillian see things his way. And Meena was right—he'd have to be patient about it.

If not? He'd scare her away. He didn't want to spend another hour without her. He prayed God would soften her heart and give him the right words. Too much was riding on the outcome. His heart. His future. His happiness.

"Babysit?" Lillian ushered Meena inside the cabin just as she'd gotten the nerve to call Brody and tell him how she felt. "Did you read my mind?"

Meena chuckled. "A mind reader I am not. I figured you've been stuck in the cabin for days, and you probably could use a break. Plus, I love Jonah."

"That makes two of us. He's napping at the moment." Lillian debated whether she should sit and chat with Meena for a while or take advantage of the opportunity and head out to find Brody. "Sonny dropped off some yummies earlier if you're hungry."

"I've been stuffing myself for days. I'm going to have to seriously embrace healthy eating after the new year." Meena dropped onto the couch and opened the tote she'd brought with her. She slid out a thick book.

"What's that?" Lillian spotted the cover of a white farmhouse.

"Oh, a new decorating book. I bought it for myself for Christmas. I like getting ideas." She flipped open to the first page. "I'll be working on Cooper's cabin next. I keep trying to talk Hayden into letting me remodel his place, but he crosses his arms over his chest and gets that stubborn glare. What the man has against new paint and a few well-placed decorations, I will never know."

Lillian laughed, and then a knock on the door made her pivot. "I'll be right back."

When she opened the door, her mouth went dry at the sight of Brody in his Stetson, unzipped coat, and sweater, jeans and cowboy boots. He rested one forearm on the doorframe and hitched his chin to her. "You busy?"

"Um…" A whiff of his cologne hit her, and she almost closed her eyes to savor it.

"She's not busy!" Meena shouted from the couch.

Brody tried to look beyond Lillian.

"Meena's here," Lillian said.

"I'm babysitting Jonah," she called.

"Good." A lazy smile curved his lips. "Come on. Let's take a walk."

A walk. Right. Brody stood on the entry mat while Lillian shoved her feet into her winter boots, pulled on her coat and stocking cap and turned to Meena. "There's a bottle ready in the fridge, and—"

"I've got this. Don't worry." Meena grinned, waving her off. "Get out of here."

Well.

Brody opened the door for her, and they made their way down the drive past the cabins.

"Beautiful day." She felt tongue-tied. She had so much to

say and couldn't find a way to start. "Merry Christmas Eve, by the way."

"Same to you. And yes, it is nice out." Was he nervous, too? This handsome, self-assured man?

They turned down the drive that led to the ranch's outbuildings. Pressure began to build inside her as they continued forward in silence. She couldn't blurt out that she loved him. Not when so much of their previous conversation had been muddled and confusing.

"I've been thinking a lot since we last talked." Brody pointed to the stables. "We're going over there."

He'd been thinking. That couldn't be good. Nor could the fact that he hadn't reached out to her in days. Her spirits sank.

Why had she thought they could have something real? Something lasting?

She'd blown it. She should have called him earlier. Shouldn't have let so much time pass.

The familiar refrains fired. *Pack your stuff. They're sending you away. Don't cry. You'll be fine. Brenda might not be here this time, but that doesn't mean you'll be on the streets.*

Lillian stumbled, and Brody caught her by the arm. "Are you okay?"

No, she wasn't okay. She no longer had a caseworker helping her make the transition from getting turned out by a family. She'd waited too long.

With a nod and a swallow, she pressed forward. He slid open the barn door for her, and it took a few moments for her eyes to adjust to the dim light. Her thoughts tumbled around her head as she stayed near his side until they reached the end of the aisle.

What now? Were they going to discuss their feelings or pretend the past two months never happened?

As her chest burned, she remembered Sonny's advice. *Tell him how you feel.*

Brody stopped in front of the end stall. The fawn came right up to him, sniffing his hand. Lillian's tortured thoughts quieted.

"Why are we here?" she asked. "Can I pet him?"

"Go ahead."

She extended her hand, and the deer smelled it and continued to stand there. She petted his forehead and neck. "He's soft."

"I thought you'd like to go with me to set him free." Brody unlatched the gate. "Would you open that door? The UTV should be ready."

"So soon? Will he be okay?" Lillian hurried to the side door a few feet away and opened it. Sure enough, a UTV with a large crate in the back was parked there. The crate's door was open. Brody carried the fawn to the crate and gently set him inside. Then he secured the door and hitched his head for Lillian to join him.

"It's time. Hop in."

She scrambled over to the passenger side and lowered herself into the seat. Held onto the handle as Brody took off. He kept the speed to a minimum, and she glanced back to check on the fawn but couldn't see much.

"Don't worry. I'm taking it slow. We don't have far to go." Brody drove along the side of one of the pastures until he reached a forested area. Then he skirted the edge of the forest and came to a stop where a yellow flag had been planted near a tree. "There it is."

"What?"

He cut the engine, got out and pocketed the keys. She joined him at the back.

"Hayden marked the way to the deer path. We'll get him in position to join his herd."

Hope for the fawn excited her, but his future worried her, too.

"What if they don't find him?" she asked as he opened the crate door and once more carried the fawn in his arms. The deer didn't fight it.

"They will. And he has good instincts. He'll know where to go."

"But a predator could attack him." She had to hurry to keep pace with his long legs.

"It could."

"I don't like this, Brody. If we let him go, we can't keep him safe."

They trudged through thick prairie grass, curled over from the cold, and dodged tree branches. Brody remained silent. Then he slowed, stopping at another tree with a yellow flag planted next to it. He set the fawn on its feet. And the little deer sniffed him, then turned to Lillian and sniffed her.

She wanted to throw her arms around his little neck and tell him it would be okay. That he could live in the stables forever where it was warm and safe. They'd feed him and love him and…

"We have to let him go, Lil." Brody's tender expression threatened to unravel all her knotted emotions. "For his sake."

"I don't want to," she whispered.

The deer bent its neck to smell the ground, took a few tentative steps away from them and then began bounding away.

"He's gone." She closed her eyes, surprised to be fighting back tears.

"He's still there." Brody took her gloved hand in his. "Look."

She turned her attention to where Brody stared. The fawn had stopped to graze.

"This is a well-traveled wildlife path. We didn't let him loose just anywhere."

"You mean the other deer come this way?"

"Every day." Brody took off his gloves and tenderly traced down her cheek. "I know you care what happens to the fawn."

She nodded, not trusting herself to speak.

"I do, too. And the right thing to do was to let him go. Just like you."

Lillian froze, her heart shrinking inside her chest. He was letting her go.

And all of a sudden she was that little girl on the porch step with all her belongings in the world next to her in a trash bag.

"I understand, Brody." She'd be brave. Courageous. Sonny had said that about her, too. "I won't make this awkward."

Brody didn't know what she was talking about or what she thought she understood, but he could guarantee she had it all wrong. *Patience.*

"When you arrived on the ranch, you needed our help," he said. "A safe, warm place to get back on your feet. Like the fawn did."

The way her eyes were darting around and her tongue was licking her lips, he doubted he was getting through to her. He took both her hands in his and waited until she looked into his eyes.

"I wanted to keep you here. In your cabin. Safe and warm. Where I could take care of you and see you whenever I wanted. But I wasn't thinking about what you needed. I was thinking about myself."

Her eyelashes fluttered.

"Lil, you've been honest with me all along. You were finding a job and a place to stay. I could only see the danger—mainly, that I wouldn't see you as much. That you'd get your own life and wouldn't need me in it."

"I will always need you in my life," she said quietly.

"Really?" He brushed her cheek with his thumb. "I know I need you in mine. I'm sorry about the other night. I'm sorry you had to rehash the pain of quitting college, of losing Rebecca. And I'm sorry you had to go through that alone. I don't want you to be alone, Lillian. Ever. I want to be your person. I want to be the one you come to when you get good news or bad. I want to be the shoulder you cry on when life gets to be too much. I want to celebrate your victories."

Her eyes glistened with love…and concerns.

"What is it?" he asked, bending to stare into her eyes. "I know you. You're worried."

"I want all that, too, but what do you get out of it?"

She still didn't get it. Still didn't understand what she brought to the table. He wrapped his arms around her and crushed her to him. Then he whispered near her ear, "You. I get you. I love you, Lillian. I love your loyalty. I love the way you listen to everything I say, even when I toss out dumb ideas. I love that you don't mind my big plans or act like I'm stupid for having them."

"I love your big plans. They're never stupid."

"See? You believe in me. That kind of blind faith—it went straight to my head. And my heart had a hard time trusting it."

"I have a hard time trusting most good things."

"That's because so much bad has come your way." He inched back slightly, cupping her face, staring into those big, beautiful eyes. "I'm not pressuring you to stay on the ranch anymore. I'm letting you go, like the fawn, because I know you'll be safe. You'll be here in Fairwood like you've said all along."

Understanding sparked in her eyes. "You thought I was just saying I'd stay. I didn't realize..."

"I've had trust issues since Rebecca."

"That's fair."

"But I'm working on them, and I finally acknowledged to myself that I had them before her, too. I was never my parents' top priority."

"You deserve to be top priority." The way her face was shining made him forget they were out in the cold.

"I love you, Lillian Splendor. I know you have your doubts. I know you compare yourself to Rebecca, and I wish you wouldn't. She was a special person, but I didn't love her because I didn't know the real her. I know you. I love you. You're as real as they come."

He stopped talking, blew out a breath and watched for her reaction.

"I love you, too, Brody." The words came out shyly. "And you don't have to let me go. I was trying to protect myself from getting hurt. And I do have something for you."

When she didn't continue, he searched her eyes. "What?"

"My heart. All of it."

He wrapped his hands around her waist, leaned forward and pressed his lips to hers. This woman. She had no idea how much he loved her. He kissed her slowly, then more persistently, enjoying the softness of her mouth against his. All of his pent-up energy and the loneliness of the past decade disappeared in an instant.

Lillian Splendor was his, and he was never going to let her go.

Chapter Fifteen

Lillian wasn't sure how much time had passed when she entered the front door of the lodge holding Brody's hand. Had there ever been a better Christmas Eve? And the celebrations were just beginning.

Meena had texted her that she was bringing Jonah to the lodge, and Lillian and Brody had taken their time before driving the UTV back to the stables. They'd walked hand in hand, talking about everything and nothing—their future and what Sonny had planned for the Christmas Eve supper. Naturally, the chef had insisted on providing a feast, but he'd been keeping the menu a secret. Lillian could eat a bowl of cereal and be happy.

Brody was hers. And she was his.

As soon as she'd taken off her coat, she moved to head down the hall, but Brody reached out and tugged her back to him. "Wait."

His eyes gleamed with appreciation for her. She loved the feeling of being in his arms. "What?"

"Meena and Hayden know my feelings for you."

She could feel her smile slip. "And?" Was he warning her they didn't approve?

"And they're going to be hugging you and making a big deal out of us being together."

"So they're happy about it?" She scrunched her nose, not sure what to think.

"Yes, they're happy. A little too happy. I don't want you to be overwhelmed by them. I know we can all be…a lot."

"That's what I love about your family. They're not lukewarm, that's for sure." She reached up on her tiptoes, sliding her hands around his neck, and kissed him. "I can handle it. I think. I've never been part of a family, so I'm not sure."

"Get prepared, then, because you'll be getting teased and tormented before you know it." He kept his hands on her waist, his face close to hers.

"Good. That means they accept me."

He claimed her lips and kissed her slowly. "If they don't, they have me to answer to."

She laughed, swatting at his chest. "Come on, let's get in there."

When they entered the living room, Kylie was holding Jonah high above her. Seth and Cooper were deep in discussion in front of the open fire in the fireplace. Meena was waving her finger near Hayden's face, and Hayden was rolling his eyes at whatever she was saying. Lillian's heart was bursting with affection for this family.

Brody kept his hand at the small of Lillian's back, and they kept moving until they reached the group.

"Hey, everyone, Merry Christmas Eve!"

The room quieted, and then they all began repeating, "Merry Christmas Eve," and hugging them. Lillian was glad Meena was the last one over. Brody's sister was brimming with excitement.

"Tell me you're a couple," Meena whispered to Lillian.

"I have an announcement," Brody said loudly, raising his hand. Everyone turned their attention to him. "Lillian and

I are officially dating. I love her." Then he glanced down at her and pulled her into his side. "I love you."

Meena squealed and started hopping up and down. Kylie carried Jonah over. "About time someone corralled Brody. And I, for one, couldn't be more thankful it was you. Now I get to spend more time with this cutie bug."

Seth shook Brody's hand. "Smartest thing you've done."

Lillian met Seth's gaze, and he nodded to her. "Welcome to the fam, Lil."

Cooper gave her a hug and welcomed her, too. Finally, Hayden came over and smiled. "You can't go wrong with this guy. He's the real deal."

"Thanks, man." Brody grinned.

"Treat her like gold, or you'll have me to answer to." Hayden's warning made Lillian giggle.

"I've got to tell Sonny." Lillian pulled away from Brody. "Be back in a few."

"Don't leave me alone too long."

"You'll survive." She laughed at his puppy eyes. "I'll be right back."

She found Sonny stirring something on the stovetop and ran over to him.

"Do you have good news?" He set the spoon on the counter and faced her.

"Yes. Brody and I are officially dating. We're in love."

Sonny hugged her. "Wonderful!"

"Did you call Josie?" She leaned against the counter as he stirred a different pot.

"I did."

"And?" She held her breath, hoping he had good news, too.

"I apologized. Wished her a merry Christmas." His sad smile tore her heart.

"She didn't take it well?"

He gave his head a small shake.

"I'm sorry." She placed her hand on his arm. "Maybe this is the first step. You'll take another. And another. And one day things will begin to heal."

"I hope so." He couldn't hide his pain, and she wished she could fix the relationship for him.

"In the meantime, you have us."

"Thank you. That's more than a lot of people have."

"Don't I know it." A look of understanding passed between them. "Now, let me help you with supper."

"No." His smile was genuine as he pointed the spoon to the archway. "Out. You know I cook alone."

She gave him a side hug and left the room. She paused at the side of the living room to take it all in. *God, thank You for leading me here. Thank You for the gift of Brody's love.*

And she thought of the fawn in the woods, and she knew the tiny deer was going to be all right.

Matching pajamas. Meena had insisted all of them—including Sonny, Lillian and even baby Jonah—wear matching pajamas on Christmas morning. Brody wasn't even as disgusted by it as he thought he'd be. Not with Lillian sitting near the girls with Jonah on her lap. He continued to shove wrapping paper in a trash bag, keeping his eyes open for any paper bits he might have missed.

"This is the best Christmas ever." Kylie sipped cocoa with whipped cream on the sectional. Meena had one knee to her chest where she sat a few feet away from Kylie.

"It is for me." Lillian's quiet words reached him, and he checked on her. He'd worried about her this morning, knowing her first Christmas without Rebecca would be hard. She'd clung to him for a while when he'd asked her how she was holding up, and he'd stroked her back as she cried silent tears.

At the moment, though, she seemed happy, so he continued cleaning up.

Seth's dog, Liverwurst, had joined Butch for a nap in front of the fireplace. Cooper was scrolling on his phone, and the back of Hayden's head had nestled into the couch. His eyes were closed.

How anyone could nap with Kylie and Meena yapping away about the beauty products they'd gotten each other, he'd never know. Satisfied he'd gotten all the scraps, he hauled the bag to the kitchen and found Sonny sitting at the table, nursing a mug of coffee. He was staring at his phone intently.

"Everything all right, Sonny?" Brody paused near the table.

The man glanced up at him, and if Brody wasn't mistaken, he looked emotional.

"It's good." He sounded choked up.

What was he supposed to do in this situation? Brody could barely handle women's emotions. He had no clue what to do with Sonny's.

"Well, we'd love for you to join us out there. You don't have to sit in here by yourself."

"I think I'll take you up on that." His smile reached his eyes. Maybe he wasn't sad after all.

Lillian came into the room. "I need another sugar cookie." She stopped short when she saw Sonny and rushed over to him, putting her hand on his shoulder. "What happened?"

Brody's mouth fell open. How did she always seem to know what was going on?

"Josie. She texted me this morning."

"She did?" Lillian's face filled with hope. "What did she say?"

"She wished me Merry Christmas."

"Oh, Sonny. That's the best news." Lillian put her arms

around the man's neck, and he held her for a long moment. Brody still felt clueless, but he was also proud that this caring woman was his.

Lillian turned to Brody with her face glowing. "His daughter wished him Merry Christmas."

"That's great, man." He held up the trash bag. "I'll just get rid of this."

Brody pivoted and sped through the kitchen to the mudroom. He set the bag down near the door and returned to the kitchen, where Lillian stood nibbling on a cookie near the big picture window. She must have sensed him come in, because she waved him over.

"Come here. Quick."

He was at her side in an instant. She pointed toward the woods. "Are you seeing what I'm seeing?"

He squinted, then he grew aware of where she was pointing. A herd of deer stood near the forest's edge, and one small fawn grazed with them.

"It's him." Lillian's voice was laced with awe, and her eyes glistened as she gazed up at Brody.

"It is."

"He found his herd."

"And you found yours." He spun her to face him and cupped her face with his hands. "I don't know what I'd do without you." He kissed her tenderly. "Merry Christmas."

"May every Christmas be as special as this one."

Epilogue

The Wyoming sunset was something. Brody rested his forearms on the porch rail of the lodge as he watched for Seth's truck to pull up. The air was cold for February, but the orange, purple and magenta streaks in the sky made up for it. He was glad Lillian and Jonah were warm and cozy in her cabin. As soon as Seth got here, Brody could move forward with his plan.

He had everything ready. The flowers. The romantic playlist. The ring.

He was proposing to Lillian, and the squad would be on hand to celebrate.

Brody had decided to wait to pop the question until they could all be together again, and the only way they would be was during their monthly meeting.

Meena had been a lifesaver throughout this process. She'd told him when his ideas were bad—and yes, she'd said, "That's the dumbest thing I've ever heard," more than once—given him better suggestions and helped him work through every detail.

He was nervous, and he was also excited. He couldn't wait for Lillian to be his wife.

Seth's truck came into view, and Brody headed down the porch steps while he parked. He waited for him to let the dog out of the back seat before bringing him in for a half embrace.

"You made it." Brody clapped his hand on Seth's shoulder, then scratched behind Liverwurst's ears.

"I did." Seth waited for the dog to return to his side. "For good."

"You don't know how glad I am to hear it. Music to my ears." Brody walked next to him back to the lodge. "You're sure about moving here?"

"Yeah, I am." Seth didn't look as tired as he had the past few times they'd been together. "I'm ready to figure out my next step."

"We'll be right here if you need a sounding board." Brody opened the lodge door and waited for him and the dog to enter before closing it. They continued through to the living room where the squad had assembled.

After everyone hugged Seth, Brody let out a whistle. "Okay. Everyone understands what's happening."

"Yes, Brody. We get it. You're getting engaged." Hayden opened his hands and gave him an eyeroll. "I don't think we need a pep talk."

He decided to ignore that. "I'm going to my cabin now. Who's watching the baby?"

Cooper raised his hand. "Kylie and I will be on baby duty."

Brody arched his eyebrows. His brother? As far as Brody knew, he'd never even held Jonah. "Okay. Thanks. Where's Meena in all this?"

"I'm working on decorations." She held some kind of glittery banner. "Hayden, you're tall. You're going to have to help me."

"Fine."

"I'm out of here." Brody checked his phone. "We'll come back in one hour. Got it? One hour."

"Will you go propose already?" Hayden pointed toward the mudroom. "You're driving me out of my mind."

Brody flashed him a glare. Then he strode out of the house and to his cabin. After changing into his best outfit, he checked to make sure everything was set. His nerves were going haywire.

Romantic music played through the speaker. Was it too loud? Too quiet?

He patted his pants' pocket. Ring box safe. Bouquets of roses in vases were on the coffee table, the counter and the end table. Were five dozen enough? He should have bought six.

There could never be enough for his Lillian.

When the knock on the door came, he startled. His heartbeat thumped, and his pulse was racing so fast, it could have outpaced a NASCAR driver.

He let Lillian inside. She stole his breath as she took off her coat, revealing a black dress and heels. Her hair fell in waves, and she looked so beautiful he could barely register what she was saying.

"Are these for me?" She'd drifted to the couch and was pointing to the roses.

"Yes." He moved to her side. "They're all for you."

"All of them?" She took in the vases around the room. "So many. Brody, that's way too many."

"You deserve all of them and more." *Focus.* He wasn't going to be smooth or suave. Didn't have it in him. He took her hand in his, and she faced him. The love in her eyes gave him courage.

"I love you, Lillian. These past months have been the best of my life. And the more I get to know you, the more I want to know you. I want to spend every day with you. I want to watch Jonah grow up and be his daddy. I'm hoping we could have a couple more kids, too. Basically, I want to spend my